THE DOCTOR'S WIFE

MILDRED RILEY

Genesis Press, Inc.

INDIGO LOVE STORIES

An imprint of Genesis Press, Inc.
Publishing Company

Genesis Press, Inc.
P.O. Box 101
Columbus, MS 39703

ISBN: 13 DIGIT : 978-1-58571-424-7
ISBN: 10 DIGIT : 1-58571-424-0
Manufactured in the United States of America

First Edition

Visit us at www.genesis-press.com
or call at 1-888-Indigo-1-4-0

In memory of Helen Gray Edmonds, Ph.D.
—M.E.R.

ACKNOWLEDGMENTS

A writer's path may be a solitary one, but my family and friends have always made it possible for me to persevere.

—M.E.R.

CHAPTER 1

"Lee, I want a divorce."

"A what?" she asked, positive she had not heard right. "A what?" she repeated, still slightly bent over, still holding the tray, as if frozen in place and time.

"A divorce. I need, *want* a divorce."

"A what?" she asked a third time, this time turning so she could look directly into his eyes. His eyes told her that he was serious—deadly, completely serious. She recoiled, as if warding off unseen blows. And so she *knew*—she had not misheard, had not misunderstood. Donovan Matthews, her husband of twenty-five years, her helpmate, the father of her children, wanted a divorce! Desperate, she struggled to make sense of the out-of-the-blue demand.

"You're kidding! You have got to be kidding."

"I'm not kidding. I want out of this marriage."

The tray was about to slide out of her grip, so she finally set it down. Any minute now, she thought, I am going to wake up from what must be a nightmare. But she knew this was no sleeping nightmare. It was real, all too real.

"Don, you must be crazy! You're not making any sense at all!"

Her voice was thick with emotion and her breathing shallow, labored. Feeling weak and dizzy, she felt her eyes burning with tears. She stared at the man she had loved for practically all her adult life. Struggling to grasp the full import of his words, she instinctively braced herself for more crushing news.

The room appeared shadowy and forbidding. She had decorated it herself. She had selected a custom-made cream-colored linen-lined damask fabric. The navy blue valances were made of the same material. She loved the feelings of serenity this room evoked in her.

Now, on this dreadful night, even the oak desk she and her children had given Don for his fortieth birthday seemed to mock her. He had called it the best gift he had ever received.

The children! How will they deal with this?

Barely able to look at Don, she slumped back against the sofa. Suddenly, she wanted to smash that desk, to chop it up and throw the pieces into the fireplace. She looked at the only man she had ever loved, had ever slept with, and the white-hot anger that seized her almost choked her. Her fists curled into hard balls and she wanted to attack this person she no longer knew.

Her mind leaped from one unsettling question to the next. *What, or who, had changed this man from a loving husband and father into a man who could turn his back on his family? What had transformed him into this virtual stranger?*

As if reading her mind, he tried to soften his next words.

"I never wanted to hurt you," he began, "or the children."

Willing her eyes to focus on him, she interrupted quickly, "It's not so much hurt, although I *am* deeply hurt . . . it's disappointment . . . finding out that the man I have loved and trusted is an unworthy man . . . a despicable liar and cheat."

His attempt at a softened approach having failed, he blurted, "Is the truth so hard to bear, Leanne? I'm telling you now, I just have to say it, I just don't want to *live* with *you* anymore!"

He now hoped that unqualified plain talk would deter further emotional outbursts from his wife. Hoping, too, that this would prove effective. All he wanted to do now was to leave.

But his few curt words had cut deeply, almost killed her. Seeing the shock on his wife's face, Don knew he had to tell her the truth, knowing full well how much pain he was inflicting upon her.

Standing in front of his desk he calmly, quietly, as if explaining a procedure to one of his patients, began an explanation, of sorts.

"I'm in love with someone else, and I want to marry her."

"So, after twenty-five years, me and your children are what . . . chopped liver . . . to be cast aside?"

She tried to keep her voice steady and controlled.

"What's really wrong with you, Don? You never indicated there was anything wrong with us. Never told me you were unhappy."

His face assumed a distant, cold look. A look she had never seen before, and she knew he was deadly serious. But how could that be? They had made passionate love the night before. There had to be something wrong. Was she responsible for this . . . this horrible crisis?

"Don," she said as calmly as she could, despite the turmoil gripping her body. She felt sick to her stomach.

"I never meant to hurt you or the kids," he interrupted, his solemn voice conveying what he hoped Leanne would see as deep regret.

She did detect a hint of remorse in his voice, but her feelings of anger, hurt, resentment were unabated.

"Can't prove it by what you've just told me," she spat out with undisguised hostility.

He heard the sarcasm in her voice, had expected it. Leanne had always been strong and she had never minced her words, so you always knew what was on her mind.

Despite her initial shock, he was confident she had the strength to face even this unimaginable upheaval in her life. Strangely enough, he found himself admiring her for her fierce attitude, not that this in any way could ease the stirrings of guilt he was feeling. As well it shouldn't.

Leanne was still a beautiful woman, he mused. Despite having had two children, she had retained the extraordinary figure of her youth. Her skin had remained soft and luminous and had a tone reminiscent of Lena Horne's in her prime. She wore her dark hair in a chin-length bob; a few strands of silver brightened her temples.

"Do I know this someone?"

"No, you don't." How was he going to tell her that a nurse in his office was carrying his child?

"Just as well. I might try to kill her."

She hated his calm, expressionless demeanor. She wanted to attack him. There he stood, calm and urbane, emotionless, the man she had loved for more than twenty-five years.

He drained the wine glass, saying, "I'll be staying at the hospital in the residents' quarters. My lawyer, Frank Jones, will be in touch."

She screamed, "By all means! Go! Get out!"

She watched her husband put on his jacket and pick up the small traveling bag he usually took to his medical meetings. What she saw was a man who had almost instantaneously become a stranger. Someone she did not know. Perhaps had never known.

His football body was what had first attracted her to him, and when she met him at a football rally she knew he was the man she would marry. How could she not love the tall, broad-shouldered college senior whose deep brown eyes, when he looked at her, made her feel that she was the only woman on the planet?

They had married right after Don finished medical school and Leanne had earned a master's degree in business.

Leanne recalled the quivering nerves that had assailed her as she stood facing Donovan Matthews that day. That wonderful day they bound their lives together and pledged to love each other "until death do us part." But it was not earth that had come between them.

She had not contested the divorce. All she wanted was their cottage at the Cape. They sold the family home, each receiving half of the sale price. She did not want alimony, as she was fully capable of supporting herself. But she had insisted that Don pay for their children's college education.

"That's the *least* you can do," she had told him.

For twenty-five years, Leanne and Donovan Matthews had led serene, fulfilling lives. She had borne his children, had helped him with his promising medical career, and had kept their home happy and comfortable. With the fateful words "I don't want to live with you anymore," Leanne's whole life had fallen apart. It was as if a giant fist had slammed down on a jigsaw puzzle and scattered pieces of her life in all directions. Would she ever be whole again? Now fifty, could she put her life back together? Should she? And where would she find the strength to do so?

CHAPTER 2

Carrying a mug of hot tea, Leanne walked into the sunny patio of the cottage on the Cape.

Sitting that day on the patio, she found herself wondering, *was it my fault? When had the change in our lives come?* The questions spun around in her mind like a top that would not stop spinning.

Never in her life had she thought of herself as being weak or needy, but after twenty-five years, a husband's unexpected request for a divorce would have thrown even the most unflappable, well-put-together woman. Surely, she thought, there are limits to being a rock.

She took a sip of her now-cooled tea and glimpsed a cardinal flying by her window, a streak of crimson reminding her that spring had arrived and that the world had *not* stopped spinning despite the unfathomable turn her life had taken.

She took one last sip of tea and set down her teacup, closing her eyes and resting her head against the back cushion. Thinking of the cardinal made her recall her children's reactions when Don called the family into the living room.

Both children had been wary, suspicious that something was amiss when they gathered together.

"Come in, come in," Don said as he took a seat in his favorite chair. Curtis and Jane joined their mother on the couch, one on either side of her.

Donovan had cleared his throat before speaking. Surprising herself, Leanne had inexplicably felt sorry for him. Where had *that* feeling come from?

"Curt, Jane, you know I love both of you, and I'm tremendously proud of you. I'm sorry to have to tell you this, I know it will be a great shock and surprise . . ."

"Dad," Jane interrupted, "are you sick?" She knew how hard her father worked. "Do you have cancer? Are you dying? Oh, Dad!" she reached out to him. But his next words caused her to sit back as if someone had knocked the wind out of her.

"I'm fine, sweetheart, but I've asked your mother for a divorce."

Curt's anger had been fierce and forceful as he had railed at his father.

"You bastard! How can you do this to us, your family?"

Curtis was the firstborn and was very close to his mother.

Jane, at twenty, was close to her father, a real daddy's girl. She had turned to her mother and demanded, "How could you let this happen? You just didn't love Dad enough!"

Curtis in turn had berated his sister with a vengeance.

"Mom did everything for all of us and you *know* it!" he had protested, glaring at his father with his fists clenched at his sides.

Leanne reached for her son's hand. Seated between her children, she knew Curtis had been stunned, was beyond belief at his father's admission.

Already a senior at Brown University, he was planning for a career as a lawyer. Jane was a sophomore at Tufts University, expecting to pursue a teaching career.

This fateful weekend at home was one they would never forget.

Leanne had felt the tension that mounted in her children: Curtis, with his fists clenched, and Jane, whose widened eyes manifested her disbelief and horror.

Leanne knew then that somehow she had to help her children get through this ordeal, and most importantly keep a strong, loving relationship with their father, no matter how difficult it might be. Don would always be their father.

᠃᠃᠃

Driving across the bridge over the Cape Cod Canal, Leanne recalled the happy times the family had shared there. But her mind went back again to so many months ago now, when her life changed.

"You never told me that you were unhappy . . ."

Don's reply, "Well, I wasn't unhappy . . . I mean, it's just that I love . . ."

She interrupted him.

"Does she have a name?"

A wry grin on his face made Leanne want to slap him.

"There's no need to be sarcastic, Lee. I thought we could handle this in a civilized manner . . ."

"You thought! You thought *wrong*! It's not every day that one's husband asks for a divorce! You come home tearing my life upside down . . . the children's, too, and expect me to be civil! So, I ask you again, who *is* she?"

Don sighed. "Her name is Alisha Morton. She's one of the nurses on my staff."

"Have you slept with her?"

"Well, er, yes."

CHAPTER 3

It had started innocently enough. First there were coffee breaks in the medical center's cafeteria.

"Ready for a cuppa?" Don had asked Alisha, his office nurse, after a protracted office visit with a difficult patient whose list of medical problems, some real, some imagined, had taxed his usual patience.

He told the patient, "Now, sir, this new medication will take care of your heart problems, I'm certain. But if you have *any* difficulties at all, please let me know."

"Yes, sir, doctor, I surely will. Thank you ever so much!"

"My pleasure, sir. Stay well."

Alisha had noticed her boss' harried look and she responded quickly to his offer.

"Yes, I would like a cup of coffee 'bout now. It has been a rather busy morning. I'll let Becky know. She'll hold the patient line 'til we get back."

At first it was just a friendship between two people who shared a work space. If anyone had asked him about the relationship as it grew into something he had not anticipated, he would not have been able to answer.

But for Alisha, it was a dream come true . . . to be noticed by a physician. All of her years as a student nurse she had dared to hope that some doctor, *any* doctor, would notice her.

She told Becky, the receptionist, "Hold the patients back. Dr. Matthews and I are going for coffee, okay?"

"Okay by me," the older woman replied. "And you watch your step," she warned.

"What are you talkin' 'bout? It's just a coffee break!"

Alisha's face reddened at her co-worker's cautionary words, and she hurried out of the office, joining the doctor at the elevator.

As they rode the elevator to reach the cafeteria on the first floor, Alisha said, "Mr. Alexander can be a handful, can't he, Dr. Matthews?"

"Sometimes, but I try to be patient with him. I know he's getting on in years, lives alone, has no family. And sometimes I wonder if he ought to be in a rehab center or a nursing home. But he's very independent, and wants 'none of that stuff.' As he once said to me, 'I come into this worl' by myself, goin' out the same way!' "

"Perhaps," Alisha ventured. "you could make a referral to a visiting nurse to just check on him. Think he would accept that?"

"Good idea, Alisha! I'll suggest it on his next visit. Please put a note in his chart so I'll remember."

"Will do, and you know, once he meets the visiting nurse he might just like her, see her as a friend, someone to call on. You know, Dr. Matthews, if you'd like, when his next scheduled visit with you comes up, I can arrange to have the nurse, him or her, come to meet Mr. Alexander. That way the relationship would begin under your recommendation and he might be more receptive to the idea."

They reached the cafeteria and went straight for the coffee urn.

"This is on me," Don said as he selected a muffin from a nearby tray.

"Oh, no." Alisha pulled a small change purse from her uniform pocket.

"You can pay next time," he said. "And besides, I owe you a consultant fee for your professional advice about Mr. Alexander."

Even the Cape cottage could not relieve Leanne of the unrelenting shock, bewilderment and dismay that bedeviled her. And why did she sometimes wonder if the failed marriage was perhaps her fault? What had she done or not done? Was it her fault that made him want out of their marriage?

Don had always been an involved parent despite the demands of an internal medicine practice. He would make time to be involved in their children's activities at school and in their various extracurricular sports. Jane was an excellent swimmer. His "little mermaid," he called her. Curtis was a "four letter man" in high school track, baseball, football and ice hockey.

She was the eldest of five and her mother had encouraged her to "set an example" for her younger siblings.

Her father had not put as much pressure on her, and she adored him.

"Don't worry . . . your brothers and sisters will do fine. You just be yourself and be happy; that's what I want for you," he had told her.

Both were gone now, killed by a drunk driver while on their way to church on Sunday. Since that time she had made it her priority to assist her siblings in any way that she could.

Facing life with courage and determination was a challenge from which she had never shrunk, and she would not stop now at this momentous event in her life. "So now the broad is pregnant and you want to do the right thing . . . that's it, isn't it? I see now, Don, that you are a very weak man. I would not have believed that of you, the man I loved."

For himself, Don was not really certain when he had become attracted to the thirty-year-old nurse. Somehow the admiration and deference she showed him helped ease the daily tension in the work situation. She seemed able to help solve patient problems, make certain that the countless drug representatives did not pester him, screened out the ones she knew he did not want to see.

After weeks of having morning coffee and/or afternoon tea with Alisha, he astonished himself by telling her, "I'm attending a medical convention in Pittsburg next month . . ."

"Oh, my God, Dr. Matthews! I'm planning to visit my parents there next month. I'd planned to ask you for time off today!"

"How about that! I didn't know you were from there."

"Yes, I am. My folks are still there. Maybe you could come to dinner one night . . . know they would love to meet you."

"That would be nice."

"I was a staff nurse at Magee Woman's Hospital at the University of Pittsburgh. Worked there for several years."

Don Matthews had no idea that his assistant had fabricated a part of her story. She was from Pittsburgh, her parents did live there, but the part about the intended visit to them was made up on the news of Don's medical meeting. When she had first seen it on his calendar, her plans were about to be put into place.

Sharla Boxford reached for the bill the server had placed on their table, but Leanne's hand closed over it.

"Uh-uh, child. I'm paying for this lunch. You drove us here, and with the price of gas it's only fair that I pick up the tab."

"You know you don't have to do that, Lee. I invited you, remember?"

"Glad you did, girlfriend. Sure good to get together again. Been so long . . ."

"I know. We both lead busy lives. Is Don coming home tonight?"

"Yes, ma'am!"

Leanne's quick response made Sharla shake her head. Grinning as she said, "You sure do love that man! Where did he go this week?"

"To Pittsburgh. Some national conference on stem-cell research. Girl, I can't wait for him to come home! And, yes, I love that man until the day I die!"

"Don't I know it! Never forget the day you two got married. I was there, you know."

She reached across the table and grasped her friend's hand.

"I was your maid of honor, and when I saw how you looked at Donovan, as if you couldn't believe what was happening, I knew right then that you were deeply in love. Could see it on your face. Believe me, kid, I was one jealous maid of honor, wishing *I* were in your shoes."

"But you and Anderson have a wonderful marriage. Done all right by each other."

"Oh, sure, we're like two peas in a pod, and we are happy. Settled in our ways, living in the afterglow of a serene, comfortable relationship."

"Nothing wrong with that, Sharla."

"No, of course not, but, well, between you and Don there's a magical spark that makes everyone envious."

"Tell you the truth, my friend, sometimes I do get to wondering myself why I got so lucky, and . . . do I really deserve to be so happy?"

Sharla gave Leanne's hand a quick squeeze and started to rise from her chair.

"Honey, don't knock the blessing. Just be happy!"

CHAPTER 4

The two friends left the restaurant together, Sharla heading to her car in the parking lot and Leanne hailing a passing cab to take her to the dealership. Her car had been recalled, she intended to pick it up and then drive to Green Airport in Providence to meet her husband's three-thirty arrival.

Leanne settled back in the cab as the driver took her to Allston to the dealer's shop. She hoped and prayed that Don's flight would be on time and they could get home to Norwood without too much traffic on Route 95. Thank God it wasn't football season, so going past the football stadium would not be a problem.

She had already prepared Don's favorite: sirloin tips with mushroom gravy, rice, salad, and strawberry short-cake. His favorite wine was in the refrigerator. She had set the table beforehand, the children were away at college, so they would have the house to themselves. She felt her face flush as she drove to the airport. It had been twenty-five years since that glorious day that Sharla brought to mind, and she remembered it clearly.

Angela Bright never varied in her morning routine. Teeth brushing first, then her shower, body lotion applied, then getting dressed. Once fully clothed, she would sit in front of her dressing table and apply her makeup. First a light foundation applied to her face, then a dusting of blush on her cheeks, then eyeshadow and lip gloss.

She went to her cousin's hair salon in Providence for hair weaving extensions. She returned often to have the necessary treatments needed to maintain proper care.

The extensions were long, silky and black, framing her olive-tinted skin. Her exotic, round, dark eyes and high cheekbones made people question her racial identity. Many thought she was from India. In fact, on hearing her clipped Jamaican accent, one physician at the medical building exclaimed, "Ms. Bright, you look like you could be a relative of mine!"

As a phlebotomist, she moved about the medical center drawing blood from patients. As she brushed her hair, she wondered what, if anything, she should do about the couple she had seen on her last trip to the Providence hairdresser two weeks ago.

Early for her appointment, she had decided to have a salad and a cup of tea at a nearby café. Her hair treatment would take hours. It would be late when she drove back to Boston, so something to eat to sustain her would be a good idea.

"I'll be right back with your order, ma'am," the middle-aged woman told her. Watching the woman walk towards the open kitchen at the rear of the restaurant, Alisha saw that her gait was faulty, as if she had pains in her feet. Probably works all day. Could be a single mother supporting her family, like her very own mother had done. Her eyes stung with unshed tears as she recalled her own mother, now dead, who had worked so hard to give Angela and her brother a decent life.

She brushed the mist from her eyes and reached into her briefcase, glad that she'd brought a book along. It would be comforting to have something to read while she waited for her lunch. It was a John Grisham novel, and she had found it to be an "unputdownable" read.

Opening her book, she glanced out of the nearby window and noticed the parking lot filling up. She realized she was lucky to have been able to get a parking space. Then she spied a couple, a older man and a young woman, walking by, talking animatedly to each other.

She stared at the man. God, it was Dr. Matthews, and he was with Alisha Morton! She quickly returned to her book, bent her head over it. Would she be spotted by the couple when they passed by her booth? *Forty miles from Boston, this lunch date must have been planned. I saw his wife in the building last week, believe someone said he was taking his wife to lunch to celebrate her being named Realtor of the Year.* Angela had heard all about the occasion later.

Her friend, Gretchen, who also worked in the lab, told her all about it. She had heard about it from a coworker.

"Imagine," Gretchen said, waving her arms in an expansive gesture, "your husband takes you shopping, buys you a French designer bag with matching shoes, a Hermes scarf, and a set of pearl earrings. Then he takes you to a spa for a full massage, body wrap, mineral bath, facial, manicure, pedicure . . . the works?"

"Oh, my God," Angela gasped.

"Hey, wait, that's not all! After all that, he takes you to the Ritz Carlton for dinner and you spend the night in the penthouse suite!"

Gretchen's eyes narrowed when she saw Angela's astonished reaction to her news.

"Can you imagine someone, *anyone*, spending *that* much money on you?"

"Can't say I know anyone like that. He must love her to death . . ."

"Or have a guilty conscience!"

CHAPTER 5

Dealing with the children's "acting out" behavior was one of Leanne's most vexing problems. Jane was particularly angry and hostile towards her mother, blaming her for not loving Don enough.

"You care more about your real estate business than you do about Dad!"

"You're wrong, my dear. I have always put your father first, even before you children, and you both know I'd give my *life* for you. This is just something that has happened. I don't have the answers, but your father does love both of you. You can be sure of that."

"Well," Jane scowled, "I still think it has something to do with you . . . to make him look at another woman . . . and," her voice choked, "to want to leave *us* and marry someone else! I'll never forgive him!"

"Don't talk like that, honey. He will always be your dad, the only one you'll ever have."

With Curtis, it was somewhat different. He was angry, furious at what he called his father's irrational weakness for having abandoned his mother for another woman.

"I don't know how you can put up with his behavior, Mom. He has no right to do this to you."

"Curtis, it's his life and he has a right to live it as he chooses."

But Curtis interrupted her, unloosing a string of epithets. "He's a coward, a wimp and a cheat. And I don't want to have anything to do with him! Ever!"

"For your sake and mine, I do wish you wouldn't feel that way. As I told Jane, he is still your father and that *is* forever."

"Not anymore! Not like you, Mom. You're a real, honest-to-goodness trooper."

She hugged him.

"That's what your father called me the night you were born. 'A real trooper.' I'll never forget that. Curtis, don't judge him. He is your dad, no matter what. Always will be."

Don had been staying at the residents' quarters at the hospital for two weeks and had not contacted Leanne. However, her lawyer had called her. Leanne had made an appointment with him for advice on the divorce procedure.

"Leanne? This is Alan Spencer. How are you?"

"Oh, I guess I'm all right. I'm still trying to put one foot in front of the other. But I'm keeping busy. The children are back at their respective schools and I'm still trying to sell houses, counsel newlyweds on the vagaries of buying their first house. And I'm seeing more and more empty nesters in their declining years trying to hold onto their homes, and even helping first-time buyers. So, yes, my days are filled. The nights . . . well, you know."

"It's very hard, I'm sure, but I want you to know I'm going to try to do my best to help you get through this."

"I appreciate your support, Alan, I really do."

"So, anyway, because of your combined salaries, the support and education of the children, the assets such as the houses, offices and all investments, I've assembled a panel to go over the agreements of the divorce."

"A panel, Alan?"

"Yes, I've pulled together a group that is experienced in divorces such as yours and Don's. They've proven to be effective in handling situations like yours."

"You do know that all I want from Don is half of the house sale, the Cape cottage, and for him to continue paying for the children's education. I don't want any alimony," she said.

"Well, Leanne, I intend to discuss all the matters relevant to considering your future, as well as the children's. Have you thought about their health care, insurance, that sort of thing?"

"To be truthful, Alan, I have not. I was so blindsided, shocked. I'm still reeling and haven't been able to focus on anything except my business. I don't know what to think, or *how* to think, if that makes any sense." She sighed audibly.

"Not to worry. We all have your best interests at heart."

An appointment was made and Leanne sat for a moment, her hand resting on the receiver. She jumped, startled when the phone rang.

"Mrs. Matthews?"

"This is Mrs. Matthews."

"My name is Becky Long."

"Oh, yes, Don's receptionist. I didn't recognize your voice at first."

"That's okay. Mrs. Matthews, and may I say I'm sorry about your . . . uh, situation. And I hope this call is not too much of an intrusion."

"Thank you, Becky."

"But I'm calling because Dr. Matthews wants you to know he'd like to stop by to pick up some clothes, personal items, and wondered what would be a good time for you."

Leanne felt her face redden with anger. *The bastard couldn't call me himself!* she thought. But then she willed herself to sound unruffled by this display of rank insensitivity, deliberately forcing any trace of anger from her voice. After all, she told herself, Becky was just a reluctant messenger. It was her husband's cowardice that had placed his receptionist in this uncomfortable position. She took a deep breath before answering, hoping that she would not sound too emotional.

"Becky, Don knows my schedule. I'm in my office from nine to five. He may come whenever he chooses."

"I'll tell him, Mrs. Matthews. Take care."

Since the awful night Don had demanded a divorce, Leanne had not slept in their room.

As soon as he had picked up his bag and headed for the front door, the reality of her situation hit her with crushing force and she had screamed, "Go! Get out! I never want to see you again! You . . . you bastard!"

She had raced up the stairs as she heard the front door slam. The tears streaming from her eyes had nearly blinded her. She had stumbled into the bedroom, where just the night before she had experienced unbelievable happiness in the arms of the man she loved. The memory of that happiness now mocked her. The sight of the bed had unleashed more tears.

Her knees weakened and she had fallen to the floor, sobbing uncontrollably at the foot of the queen-sized bed. She had clutched the bedspread, pulling it toward her, trying to wrap it around her trembling body. Smelling Don's cologne on the bedding, she had yanked the coverlet off her body as if it were contaminated with a toxic substance.

She did not know how long she had been on the floor, but she remembered rising to her feet, still shaky. But her anger rose, too, unbidden, as she began to tear the bed apart.

Pillows, sheets, blankets formed a disorderly pile on the floor. Impulsively, she began to stomp on the pile, she began to see Don's face amid the bedclothes. "Son of a bitch!" she sobbed. "How could you do this to me!"

That night she knew if she had owned a gun, she might have used it. On whom, she did not know, but surely someone. She felt she was at the end of her life.

CHAPTER 6

Leanne never again slept in the master bedroom. She removed everything that belonged to her to the guest room at the opposite end of the second floor. She had a full bath near the room, which had been designed to meet the needs of her parents' use when they would visit. Now they were dead, she had only her siblings, but they all lived out of state. There was no one.

After the call from Becky Long she was glad that she had abandoned the bedroom. *Let Don see the chaos, the confusion he has brought to my life.*

She felt unable to face the world. She was losing weight, having difficulty sleeping and was constantly trying to make sure what had happened to her marriage. She still had to deal with periods of anger and hate at being left behind, not understanding how one could love and hate someone at the same time.

The day after the divorce bombshell, telling her secretary, she had called in to her office, "Sick with the flu. Anything important, please fax or e-mail me."

"Of course. Hope you feel better. Anything I can do, let me know."

"Thank you. I'm just not able to come to the office right now," she said, coughing. "Don't want to infect anyone."

"All I ever wanted was for him to love me," Leanne sobbed in Sharla's arms.

"Girlfriend, why didn't you let me know? I'd have been here straight away!"

"I know, Sharla, I know. But I've been in such a state."

"You never knew he was involved with someone?"

"That's why I'm so upset! Don never changed toward me or the children! The only thing, now that I look back on it, was he seemed to be attending a lot more conferences . . . you know, medical meetings out of town. But he always came home, was enthusiastic about the new things he'd learned . . . but . . ."

"You don't need to spell it out, honey. I get the picture."

"Sharla, who told you?"

"It was Curtis. He called me, asked me to check on you, is worried about you."

"I might have known. He has always been concerned about me. Don always said he was more my son than his, although they always got along well together. That is 'til now. Curtis is furious at his dad."

"So he told me, Leanne, and he is really worried. You know you've lost weight?"

" 'Bout twenty pounds, I guess."

"And from the dark circles under your eyes," Sharla observed, "you're not sleeping well, either."

"Sharla," Leanne said to her friend as they sat together at the kitchen table sharing coffee and the blueberry muffins Sharla had brought.

"Yes, hon?"

"How is it that I can still *love* Don as well as *hate* him? I don't understand the mixed emotions I'm feeling."

"I'm not sure. Think somewhere I read that romantic love and hate are somehow linked in the brain. I'm not sure, but I do believe it is possible."

"I can tell you one thing, going back and forth between the two feelings is really hard. And, you know, I lived longer with Don—twenty-five years—than I did with my parents. Left home at eighteen for college."

"Have you made any plans?"

"Yes. The house is up for sale, and I do have a lawyer . . . told Don he'd have to pay the kids' college tuition. And I don't want alimony."

"Why not?

"Sharla   ." Leanne's voice cracked, and she could hardly say the tormenting words."Sharla, Sharla, the . . . girl is *pregnant*!" she cried, throwing her arms up in the air in a gesture of defeat. "Did you *hear* what I said? *Pregnant*! At fifty, Don is going to be a new father!"

"But, Lee, you deserve something!"

Despite her tears, Leanne managed a wry, lopsided grin.

"Not to worry, honey, I've already *cleared* out the joint bank account. He's going to agree to the sale of some of our investments. I'll get half of the sale of the house. I have my real estate business. And I'll own the cottage. Want that for the children."

"But are you sure you are going to get a fair shake out of this marriage? After all," Sharla persisted, "you gave this man twenty-five years of your life! *Twenty-five!* That's no stroll in the park!"

Leanne nodded. "I know, but I almost feel as if I would be seeking pay for services rendered. And girl, that's not a good feeling, not at all."

"I know it's not good, but you must be practical. There's his Social Security pension. You may be entitled to some of that. Any annuities . . ."

"My lawyer has told me that he has to assemble a panel of professional experts to sort out all of those things."

"Well, that's good. I'd hate to think that you would have to go it alone."

"I do trust Alan. I'm depending on him to see me through this . . . mess."

CHAPTER 7

The call came to Don a few minutes before he was to see his first patient.

"Yes, sir!" he responded to the deep voice of the president of the medical association. "How may I help you, sir?"

"Please come to my office at ten. I have something to discuss with you."

"I'll be there," Don said. He sat still, his hand on the receiver, and stared out the window of his office. His view of the manicured grounds, the blooming forsythia, the delicate pinks of the magnolias usually relaxed him. But today he sensed it was not medical matters that Dr. John Alexander wanted to talk about.

He thought, *My personal life has nothing to do with my professional life. I'll have to let him know this at the outset. In fact, I insist that he see it that way.*

As he sat there thinking, he recalled how everyone always thought that he and Leanne were the perfect couple. He thought so, too, at first. Leanne was attractive, smart, witty, capable and seemed solidly grounded in what she wanted out of life. He adored her, admired her, felt lucky to love such a wonderful person who loved him and put him first.

But somehow his life with Leanne had become routine, although they both enjoyed their sexual life, which lately seemed to have lost the spontaneity they had once had. They did enjoy the moments whenever they occurred.

Don had noticed, too, how quickly Leanne left their bed instead of remaining in his arms as he wanted her to do.

Something about "cleaning up." But he thought it was rather an opportunity to "wash him away."

Now it had become a humdrum, mundane matter-of-fact existence. No longer glorious, excited lovers. They had become more like companions, rearing their children, pursuing their separate careers, earning income for the support and welfare of the family.

He thought about Alisha and the immediate sensation he felt in his quickening groin alerted him. He wanted her, loved her. He had to admit that initially the attention of a younger woman had excited him. And she did not look at all like Leanne.

Tiny, about five feet tall and weighing perhaps a hundred and ten pounds, she had a glowing cocoa brown skin that made him want to touch her. Her figure was neat and trim. Because she played tennis, her arms and legs were well-toned.

She wore her dark hair in a sleek chin-length bob that swirled gently around her face. To Don, she was like a breath of fresh air. She had brought a newness, a refreshing aura that he no longer saw in his wife.

He found himself looking forward to seeing her every day, sharing their coffee breaks. And he noticed her absence whenever she took a day off.

After he'd seen his nine a.m. patient, Don informed Becky Long that he would be away from the office around ten.

"Fine, Doctor. I'll hold the patient line until you get back."

"Thanks."

He took the elevator to where the association's fourth floor offices were located; billing, conference room, and the corporate offices were situated around a central lounge area. Comfortable chairs, tables with lamps, periodicals on a coffee table in the center, plus a wall-mounted television set all helped visitors relax while waiting to be called into one of the various offices.

John Alexander was a surgeon, the founder and president of the Atlantic Medical Associates. He had been a running back for a National Football League team and when his contract with the team expired, he enrolled in a medical school.

Tall, about six feet, four inches, he commanded a strong presence in the medical group.

Don Matthews, an associate for ten years, was one of the organization's most productive members. His practice had a larger roster of patients than any other practitioner.

He entered the president's outer office, well decorated with soft beige walls, matching linen draperies at the windows at the opposite ends of the room, and various seascape watercolors on the walls. The furniture was leather chairs and a leather sofa behind a coffee table covered with carefully arranged magazines. It was a room meant to signify confidence. Don knew the man's professional credentials and football memorabilia were to be found in the inner office. A room that also spoke of confidence.

The president's secretary greeted him as he entered the reception room.

"Good morning, Dr. Matthews. How are you?"

"Fine, thank you," he said to the secretary.

"He's expecting you. You may go in."

Don tapped lightly on the door, heard a man's voice say, "Come in. Yes, Don, come in! How are you?"

Dr. Alexander stood up behind his desk and extended his hand.

Don grasped the offered hand with a firm handshake, hoping to convey his position in the upcoming confrontation.

"I'm fine, fine," Dr. Alexander said. "Like some coffee? Drink? Have a seat," he pointed to a chair.

"No thanks, John, I don't have much of my time . . . have patients waiting."

Maintaining eye contact with John Alexander, who remained seated, and speaking in a controlled, firm voice, Don was determined to make his position clear.

"First of all, John, I'm assuming you called me in here because of certain rumors you may have heard."

"Well, I . . ."

"Okay, before you go any farther, let me clarify something. What I'm guessing you heard is not a rumor. My wife *has* agreed to a divorce and I *am* involved with another woman and plan to marry her as soon as the divorce is final. Now, despite the fact that this is all *personal*, I am telling you so that you will have firsthand knowledge of the facts."

"Thanks for the clarification, Don, but let me say that as an officer of this association, I am duty-bound to protect its interests, which includes looking into anything that could possibly negatively impact those interests. Federal laws apply to everything we do, including personal interactions. And so my inquiry is *not* personal; it is part of my professional responsibilities. I hope we are both clear on that."

"Yes, we are, and I hope my intentions are clearer now," Don responded.

"I do believe they are, and thanks for coming in, Don," Dr. Alexander said, signaling that the meeting was over.

CHAPTER 8

Looking back, Leanne did have a vague sense of a slight change in their relationship.

She first noticed it when she picked him up at the airport. Usually he would be excited about the medical advances he had learned about, anxious to share the experience with her, but not that day, she later recalled.

She had been so glad to see him. She rushed into his arms. He hugged her, saying, "Good to be home. I'm bushed!" He threw his bag and briefcase into the back seat of the car, climbed into the passenger side seat, then he leaned over to kiss her.

"Good conference?" Leanne had asked as she moved the car forward onto the exit ramp.

Don wiped his face with both hands as if to erase the weariness and stress he was feeling. He took a deep breath before he answered her.

"It was okay."

"Learn a lot of new material?"

"Not really. Rather disappointing . . . not a lot of groundbreaking ideas. Only a few fresh concepts for the usage of stem cells. Quite a bit of info on laws . . . that kind of thing."

"Sorry you were disappointed, Don. You usually get so much out of these conferences."

"I know, but sometimes . . . well, some are better than others. Really thought I'd get a lot out of this one, but . . ."

Turning to face her, he'd asked, "The kids all right?"

"Yes, they're fine. Might be home this weekend. At least Jane will be, not sure 'bout Curt . . . something about a project he's working on."

"I understand how that is. Be good to see both of them."

He'd puffed out his cheeks and let out a long, drawn-out sigh. Leanne took a quick look at her husband.

"You feeling all right, Don?"

"Just tired. Long hours sitting in meeting halls, tiresome at times, even with coffee breaks."

"Well, we'll be home soon and dinner is almost ready. You probably want a shower and a good night's rest in your own bed."

Concentrating on her driving, she had missed the guilty look that came over Don's face.

"Great dinner, Leanne. As usual, you're one *fine* cook."

"Go on up; I'm going to clean up things around here."

"Bring the wine when you come. As tired as I am, need something to take the edge off."

"Will do, not to worry," she'd replied.

While storing leftovers in the refrigerator, scraping pots and pans and placing them and the rinsed tableware into the dishwasher, she remembered thinking how happy she was to have her husband back home. *Can't wait for a fantastic night of loving! A week is too long!*

Her chores finished, she had taken a bottle of wine from the refrigerator and tucked it under her arm.

Picking up the glasses, she'd raced up the stairs. As she reached the top of the stairs, she could smell the soap fragrance from her husband's shower lingering in the air. *My man is waiting for me!*

Leaving the wine and glasses on the hall table, she'd hurried into the bathroom, washing her face, brushing her teeth and putting on a pricey nightgown she had purchased just for this night. It was white silk, cost a pretty penny from the top lingerie shop in town, but she didn't care. It was high waisted and fell in deep folds. She had almost felt like a bride, hoping Don would see and treat her that way.

With the cool, silk folds cascading down her eager, excited body, she thought, *You nut! You've been married twenty-five years!* Picking up the wine and glasses from the hall table, she entered the dark room, expecting that Don would be sitting up, probably reading, waiting for her. But his back was turned to her. He was fast asleep.

Leanne remembered being dismayed and disappointed as she slipped into the bed. She had nestled against his back and stroked his arm. His body was warm, firm, but he did not stir. She kept caressing his arm. Feeling a slight movement, she whispered, "Go back to sleep, honey. It's all right, go back to sleep."

He groaned and slowly turned to face her. He did not open his eyes, but he kissed her.

"Love, Lee," he murmured sleepily. She continued to caress him. Then he fitfully flung his arm across her body. She held him as he began to snore loudly. *This man is exhausted! What a week he must have had.*

CHAPTER 9

Friendly and cordial, Alisha Morton's parents were pleased to meet their only child's friend . . . a physician.

"Pleasure to meet you," John Morton said, shaking Don's hand. His hand was firm and strong. This did not surprise Don, as Alisha had told him that her father was a retired steelworker. He had reddish-brown hair, and a graying, well-trimmed beard, reminding Don of the late comedian, Redd Foxx.

"Please, sir," he said, "may I introduce you to my wife?"

A tiny woman, Don could see the mother-daughter resemblance to Alisha. Mrs. Morton's spoke in a subdued voice, "I'm happy to meet you, Doctor. Welcome to our home."

Leaning forward, Don pecked her cheek. "Thanks, Mrs. Morton."

"You are welcome anytime," she said.

During the introductions, Alisha stood close to Don, smiling broadly. She turned to her father.

"Dad, why don't you show Don around the house? It's his pride and joy," she told Don.

"It's beautiful."

"Come on along. I'll give you a tour. I know the womenfolk have last-minute details for our dinner."

Mr. Morton led Don from the oak paneled hallway into a living room on the left.

A medium-sized room with a bay window overlooked a side porch. A large red plush sofa with several black and gold pillows had been placed near a red fireplace.

On a coffee table in front of the sofa were magazines, several glass ashtrays, as well as four wine glasses on a silver tray.

Queen Anne chairs, a wooden rocker, a few tables with lamps added to the homey, friendly feel of the room, easing some of the tension Don had been experiencing.

"Here's our dining room," Mr. Morton announced as he opened a pair of wooden doors that separated the two rooms.

Hardwood floors and a gleaming mahogany table set with candles, flowers, and damask linens, with a companion mahogany buffet with an ornate silver tea set, spoke to Don of the Mortons' pride in the elegant atmosphere of their home.

As if to confirm Don's perception, without apology Mr. Morton told his guest, "We were the first black family to move into this part of the city. Now there's a lot of black families here, but from the outside you'd never know it, would you?"

"No, I wouldn't."

"Folks take pride in their property. Most have made lots of improvements. Now even some folks of the other persuasion are moving back."

"That so?"

"Yep. Want to be back here in the old part of the city, close to downtown businesses, you see."

"That's interesting, sir."

"Right. Change is always coming. And when you're dead, they're throwing dirt in your face, so you may as well live life to the fullest, I say."

"You're right, sir. Today is all you have, so make the most of it."

"You got that right, son!"

When they moved through the kitchen, Alisha was making a large salad and her mother was at the oven, basting a large turkey.

"Sure smells good in here," Don said, following his host out the backdoor to an enclosed porch. "I believe home cooking is the best."

"Wait till we get to eatin'," Mr. Morton said. "You're in for a treat, my man!"

He followed the older man out to a glassed-in porch with bamboo chairs and a sofa, with color-splashed cushions and pillows. The late sun was filtering through the windows. The room was warm and pleasant.

"We'll wait out here. The womenfolk will call us when they're ready."

Then he asked, "How long have you known my daughter?"

"Alisha has been on my staff for, oh, I would guess three or four years. I'm not sure."

"Good nurse?"

"The best, Mr. Morton. Keeps everything running smoothly."

"Always was a hard worker. Once she sets her mind to do something, there's no stopping my daughter."

The pride on the man's face was not lost on Don. The man was proud of his only child . . . and rightly so.

"So, tell me, what kind of doctor *are* you?"

"I'm what some people call a primary physician or internist. Most of my patients have medical problems: high blood pressure, heart disease, diabetes. That sort of thing."

"Probably old people like me," Mr. Morton chuckled.

"Well," Don replied, "we try to do all in our power to keep folks like you well. You seem to be in good shape, sir."

The older man sighed, and Don sensed that there was trouble on his mind.

"Expect you've noticed how quiet my wife is . . ."

"Well, I did, but thought maybe shyness was part of her nature, and you know meeting someone new is usually uncomfortable for shy people."

"Oh, no, Maribel was always a lively one. Had to run to keep up with her. But it was my daughter who noticed the change. Expect that's why she tries to get home as often as she can. Said her mother ought to be seen by a doctor."

"And?"

"Some sort of memory loss, they said, after they put her through a lot of tests."

"I'm sorry to hear that, sir. Is she on medication?"

Responding to the sympathy in Don's voice, he pointed to the gold wedding band on Don's finger.

"I see that you are a married man, have a wife, so you *know* that when your better half is ailing, you feel it, too. In fact, wish it could be you and not her. Right?"

Don nodded soberly.

"Doc, I'm afraid *no* medicine is goin' to fix what's wrong with my wife."

"I'm very, very sorry. Hope having me here for dinner . . ."

"Oh no, that's no problem. She's happy to do this . . . makes her feel useful."

Shaken by the news of Maribel's diagnosis, Don wondered. Already he knew he was drawn to Alisha, but for the moment had not a clue as to how things were headed.

As if by some kind of parental intuition, Alisha's father spoke, his eyes directed at his dinner guest.

"Dr. Matthews, please don't hurt my daughter."

Before Don could answer, Alisha stood in the doorway. "Dinner is ready," she smiled.

As he stood up to go into the dining room, he said quietly, "Never, Mr. Morton. Never!"

Don said he would take a taxi back to the hotel, but Alisha had told her parents that she and her long-time friend, Julie, had planned to spend the night together. "A sleepover, like we used to have. Some catching up to do, so it won't be a problem for me to drive Don back to his hotel. I can borrow your car, okay, Dad?"

"By all means; no problem."

CHAPTER 10

After helping her mother with the after-dinner chores, Alisha ran upstairs to change her clothes.

Accustomed to seeing her in a white lab coat or a colorful printed pants outfit at the office, when she came back down Don was stunned by how wonderful she looked.

Her hair was curled about her face in a pixie-like style. She was wearing a pair of black slacks with a beige silk blouse that was printed with a black paisley pattern. She wore black patent-leather sandals and large gold hoop earrings, a light wool black jacket folded over her arm. A black leather shoulder bag completed her outfit. At the bottom of the stairs she placed a small overnight bag on the floor.

"Now don't forget, Dad, I'll be spending the night at Julie's. We've got a lot of catching up to do."

"One of my oldest friends," she explained to Don.

"Well, I don't want to put you to any trouble. Can just as well take a taxi."

"Gosh, no. It's right on my way to Julie's. Right, Dad?"

"That's right. Pass right by the hotel on your way to Julie's place."

Alisha kissed her mother, and turning to her father, said, "Dad, thanks so much for letting me use your car."

"No problem, honey."

"And, Dad, should you need me, use my cell phone number. That way you can always reach me . . . in case."

"Don't fret yourself about us. Have a good time at Julie's. Tell her we said hi."

"Will do."

Don picked up Alisha's bag and they made their way out to the car parked in the driveway.

"You don't have to do this," Don insisted. "I can get a cab back to the hotel."

"I'm going in that direction anyway. May as well take the ride."

"If you don't mind, then okay."

He helped her into the driver's seat and then settled himself in the passenger seat.

As Alisha drove toward the city's center, she said, "Thanks for coming tonight. My parents always like having company, happy when I bring friends home."

"They're a wonderful couple. Can see they are devoted to each other and they raised you to be a wonderful young woman, Alisha."

Alisha Morton was not about to make any mistakes. She wanted Don Matthews and knew that if she followed her plans carefully, she would get him. He was everything she wanted: a successful career, good looks, an enviable position in society. If she could somehow make herself more valuable to him as she had done in his office.

"Things run very smoothly," he'd once told her, "when you are on duty."

"Thanks, Don, for saying that. I am concerned, especially about my mother, and my father, too. He has hypertension, and watching over my mother doesn't help that, either."

Watching her skillfully negotiate the city streets, he said, "You're a very good driver, Alisha."

"Thanks, my dad taught me to drive when I was fifteen. Got my license when I was sixteen and a half . . . been driving ever since," she said, grinning at him.

There was something about her that made him certain that she always knew what she was doing. She certainly was that way in the office: alert, a hard worker. He had begun to rely on her.

But what exactly was he feeling towards her? He truly loved Leanne. But why was he so attracted to his office nurse?

Having exhausted the usual small talk, they sat in a kind of expectant silence as they drove to Don's hotel. Looking straight ahead, he took refuge in focusing on something safe—anything but what was *really* on his mind. *Tomorrow's session ends at eleven in the morning, giving me time to check out and make my flight to Providence Green Airport, where Leanne will be waiting.* But indirectly reminding himself that he had a *wife* did little to dampen his overheated libido.

For her part, Alisha spent *her* silent moments glancing over at Don. Because he kept his eyes focused on the traffic ahead, she could see only his profile in the semidarkness. But that did not matter, as she had retained a mental picture of every inch of his face. Never had she seen a more handsome man.

He had a broad forehead and softly expressive dark-brown eyes. His black hair was cut short and brushed back from his forehead, and his smooth café au lait skin was tempting—practically an invitation to touch. And that is what she longed to do.

Don the doctor had retained the athlete's body of Don the football player, having maintained well-defined muscles and a supremely confident bearing. Alisha wondered what it would be like to see that body bare.

The thought unsettled her, and she had to swerve to keep her father's car directly behind the car ahead.

Don asked, "You all right?"

"Sorry 'bout that. I'm just thinking about my mom."

The lie came easily, and she knew Don would accept it at face value.

"It's so hard having an ailing parent, especially with a degenerative disease. My wife lost both her parents at the same time . . . an accident, and it was a hard time for her . . . for all of us, really."

"I can imagine."

"You have any close relatives you can call on for help, say, in an emergency?"

" 'Fraid not. I have a cousin who lives in Alabama, but we've never been close . . . can count on one hand the number of times I've even met her."

"That's too bad."

Alisha didn't like the somber tone the conversation was taking and tried to lighten the mood.

"Yes, it is, but well, 'that's the way the mop flops,'" she said lightly.

"I know, but if there's ever anything *I* can do, don't hesitate to let me know."

"Gee, thanks, I appreciate that."

"You know, Alisha, I mean it."

"I know, and it helps to hear you say that."

She slowed the car, telling him that his hotel was the next street over.

"That was quick. And I want to thank you very much for an enjoyable evening. It was really great, meeting your folks . . ."

"They were happy to have you. I've been lucky to have them . . . owe them a lot. Well, here we are," she said cheerfully. "Signed, sealed and delivered."

"Right, and I thank you for your time and consideration."

"You're very welcome."

Don unbuckled his seat belt and leaned over to kiss her cheek. "Good night, Alisha."

He got out of the car but stopped short of closing the door.

"Oh, just remembered. Two days ago there *was* a session on Alzheimer's disease. Quite a bit of information, new clinical trials, that sort of thing. Might be helpful to you. Wait here and I'll run up to my room and get the material I picked up."

"I'd like that. Never know, something new might be coming down the pike. Let me park the car and I'll come up with you to get the material. You don't have to come back down. I'll grab it and be on my way to Julie's."

"Okay," he said, closing the car door and walking the few steps to the front of the hotel.

While waiting in the dark, he tried to remember what he had done with the monograph. He remembered picking it up and shoving it into his briefcase, but that was two or three days ago, and he had cleaned out his briefcase for new material.

As he stood there in the dark, he had another troubling thought. *What was he thinking and . . . what was he expecting?* Suddenly he knew, and his body was insisting he wanted to make love to her. This was beyond reason, beyond thought. It was a primal need for sexual fulfillment, but his body hungered for it.

He watched as he saw her cross the driveway toward the hotel's front door. He had such a strong feeling of certainty. It was right, he told himself, that she should come to him. Any lingering thoughts of decency, morality, fidelity fled his mind completely. He had to touch her; the urge to do so had been building from the moment of their "coffee" mornings.

As they walked to the bank of elevators to reach his room on the third floor, he warned her, "It may take me some time to find the article. Not sure where I put it. But I do know it's somewhere among my papers."

"That's okay."

"Well, I don't want to keep you from getting to your friend. It's getting late."

"I'll call her, let her know I'm on my way. No problem at all. This is a very nice hotel," she said as they walked to his room.

"It is. I've been comfortable here."

At Room 308 Don inserted the magnetic card into the door lock, opened the door, and stepped back for her to enter.

As she entered, she noticed that the bathroom was on the right, a closet on the left. Moving down the short corridor a few steps led into the bedroom.

The walls were painted a soft beige color and the draperies at the picture window were a robin's egg shell blue with a gold and peach floral pattern.

Alisha went to the window and looked out at the dark night. The area was illuminated by several security lights that revealed she was looking at the parking lot.

"Oh, this room faces the front. I can see my car parked right out there."

"So it does," he said, joining her at the window. Then he closed the blinds, and turned on a table light, pointing to a dark blue velour armchair beside the table.

"Here, Alisha, sit while I look for the article I told you about," he said, pointing to a dark blue velour armchair near the table.

Then he shrugged off his suit jacket, tossed it on the head of the bed. He then removed his tie, loosened his collar and rolled up his shirt sleeves—all of which she watched with growing excitement.

She continued watching him as he began looking around the room again looking for the article. Taking in the large king-sized bed, the plush dark blue rug, the French armoire that housed the television set, she began to wonder, could this be the night she gets Matthews? At least physically she was where she wanted to be, alone with the man she loved. His marital status was of no concern to her. Not at the moment, anyway. She would deal with that when it became necessary.

Then she heard him say, "Found it! Think you'll find it interesting."

"Thanks, Don," she said as she took the stapled pages from him. She read aloud, "New Approaches to the Treatment of Alzheimer's Disease. This should be interesting . . ."

"Look," he interrupted her, "maybe we can have a glass of wine before you leave. There's some real nice sherry in the refrigerator."

She settled back in the chair. *Things were going her way.*

CHAPTER 11

When he went into the bathroom, hot, perspiring profusely, Don knew he had reached a crossroad in his life. Was it possible to love two women? Leanne was his wife, the mother of his children, his partner in life, his friend of twenty-five years.

But what about this passion he was feeling for Alisha? Whenever he was near her he felt alive, alert, capable; and he had a strong sense of well-being in her presence.

How could he, should he? Indeed, should he throw away twenty-five years of marriage?

He took off his wilted shirt and removed his trousers. Then he washed his face with cold water, toweling himself dry. He pulled on a pair of sweatpants and a Patriots football jersey labeled Tom Brady, number twelve. While brushing his teeth and then swishing some mouthwash around in his mouth, he was actually aware that he was facing a pivotal moment in his life.

He clicked off the bathroom lights and found the bedroom in the darkness.

"Alisha? Where are you?"

"Right here," she answered, her voice soft, inviting.

"Right where?"

His eyes began adjusting to the darkness. Then he saw her; she was in the bed.

"What . . . what are you doing in my bed?"

"Waiting."

"Waiting for what?"

"For you. Who else?"

"Girl, Alisha, you must be *crazy!*"

"I am. Crazy about you. Now come to bed, I've been waiting too long as it is for this night. I love you, Don. You must know that."

She wanted him, he thought, and any remnant of reason vanished. His body was reacting to a sexual invitation that rendered any restrictions or doubts from his mind.

He remembered something from one of his medical school classes in Human Sexuality: something about hormones, testosterone levels, chemicals like dopamine, serotonin, and the like. But tonight he was not thinking or feeling like a physician. Tonight he was a man.

Before getting into the bed, Alisha had opened the drapes and soft moonlight filtered into the room.

"Alisha! I'm married, I can't do this!"

"Yes you can, and you know you want to."

As if he had no will at all, he found himself drawn to the side of the bed. Alisha was sitting up, her head against the headboard. He was stunned by the lovely satin luster of her bare arms and shoulders.

Staring at her, feeling the tense agony of an uncomfortable erection. He needed, wanted release from the painful sensation he was experiencing.

Reacting to her seductive smile, he tore off his clothes and slid into the bed. She was naked. Her boldness thrilled him, and her lovely warm body excited him.

She wagged a forefinger in front of his nose.

"Aren't you forgetting something?"

With a blank look, he said, "Forgetting?"

"Under your pillow, my dear."

She watched with amusement as he retrieved the silver packet, and prepared himself. As he stretched out beside her, feeling the seductive heat that rose from her body, he relaxed. All was well.

Alisha snuggled close to him.

"I knew it," she whispered.

"Knew what?"

"That we'd be a perfect fit. Make love to me, Don."

Her touches were gentle, her caresses light and feathery, but they sent flames of desire all through his body. He kissed her softly, tenderly. Then the demands of passion overcame him, and he sought the sweetness inside. Her responsive moans told him now that frissons of passion were engulfing her body.

He cupped his left hand around her delicate breast, its firm nub responding like a hard marble under his thumb.

Alisha gasped from the exquisite sensation she was feeling. She had been aching for this all these months. It was what she needed from this wonderful man she loved. Her mother had always said, "When the right man comes along, you'll know." But it was not her fault that Don had married the wrong woman. At last everything was right . . . as it should be.

Don began to kiss her closed eyes, her nose, planting delicate kisses along her neck, her ears. She trembled in his arms, and when his mouth covered the firm nub of her other breast, she thought she was going to die. She began to pant, her breath coming in hushed gasps. Waves of passionate excitement flooded her body. She never had a moment like this before. Her need for immediate fulfillment was so great, a tumultuous feeling rose from the core of her body.

Instinctively, she widened her legs and gasped frantically as Don entered her body. Losing all control, she made every effort to satisfy the demanding needs of her body. Swinging her legs over her lover's back, she gripped him tightly, much as a drowning victim clings to a rescuer.

They lay together entwined until their breathing slowed and their heart rates returned to a normal rate.

Alisha spoke first, her voice husky with emotion. "Thank you, Don. I love you, love you . . ."

"Shh-h-h, I know, I know."

She curled her body up against his, making him all the more aware that she, unlike Leanne, had not fled their lovemaking nest. He lay there for almost an hour, thinking, *I've been unfaithful to my wife after all these years. How did I let this happen? What's wrong with me?*

Alisha slept soundly, so Don eased out of the bed. He went into the bathroom. He needed to shower. He couldn't let this happen again. Just couldn't!

He washed his hair, finished his shower, dried himself with one of the hotel's thick towels, then shaved and brushed his teeth. He put on the hotel's white Turkish bathrobe, then combed his hair. He lectured himself, *You must not get back into that bed!*

When he moved quietly back into the room, he immediately noted a change.

The bedside table lamp was lit, but the bed was empty. He rushed to the picture window just in time to see Alisha getting into her father's car. As if on cue, she turned and waved up at the window. She got into the car and drove off. He glanced at the clock radio on the bedside stand. It was three-thirty. *You are such a dumb bunny. The girl planned this all along and you got sucked right in! What a fool! She set a trap and you stepped into it.*

Since he was already up, he decided he might as well get a head start. Throwing the bedspread over the now offensive bed, he began to pack. He removed shirts, ties, socks and underwear from the bureau drawers and packed them into his carry-on bag. Then he cleared the bathroom of his toiletries.

He had placed a pair of gray slacks, a sport shirt, and a navy blue blazer on a hanger, planning to be dressed casually for the morning's half-session and for the flight home.

After he had done that, he decided to watch the morning news.

By seven-thirty he was dressed and on his way to breakfast, and then on to checkout. After settling his bill, he returned to his room, sat down, thinking over the events of the past week.

How could he have been so befuddled? He, a board-certified physician, a man with the largest roster of patients in his group practice, a doctor who cared for and managed the medical problems of hundreds of patients. How could he have been so stupid, so captivated by

Alisha that he became unfaithful to his wife, the mother of two wonderful children? Leanne had been his anchor, his friend, the woman he loved.

Sitting alone in the room, he found it difficult to remember the previous night's events. It was as if he did not want to remember.

He leaned forward in his chair, his elbows on his knees, his head in his hands.

Alisha had used him for her own selfish gratification. He could see that now. But what of his own selfishness? After all, there had been no gun at his head. What made him do it? What base urges had prompted him to falter, to deny his marital vows?

You did it because you wanted to, he thought to himself. *You were lustful, flattered that you could meet the sexual needs of a young woman and enjoy the experience. Made you feel like a young stud. Now what? No more, no more. That's it.*

He went into the bathroom to wash his sweaty face. As if seeking to put himself back into his normal life, he decided to telephone Leanne.

"Yes, Lee, it's me. Be home this afternoon, like we planned. Right, Greene Airport, at three."

Her excited, cheerful voice only increased his feelings of guilt.

"Oh, Don, I'll be *there*. Don't worry!"

Thinking about his wife made him feel ill. He felt trapped, caught, almost unable to think straight. He was not accustomed to feeling this way. He did not like it. Not at all.

CHAPTER 12

Leanne rose early the next morning, sensing how travel-weary her husband seemed the night before—apparently too tired to even make love to her.

It was Sunday and she was making a brunch-style breakfast. She quickly got to work readying the mix for blueberry muffins. Once the muffins were in the oven, she opened a can of beef hash and spread it on a flat baking dish.

She had already placed a bottle of champagne to chill in the refrigerator, along with the orange juice and two glasses.

She next set the kitchen table for two. When the children were not at home, she and Don used the kitchen for breakfast and the dining room for a leisurely evening meal, usually ending with wine in the family room.

She opened a can of baked beans and would heat them in the microwave when Don came down. *I've never seen him so tired. Must have been an exhausting week.* Despite herself, her mind had returned to last night.

The timer signaled that the muffins were baked, so she removed them from the oven and put them on a wire rack to cool. She placed the rack on the granite countertop.

The last thing that she did was to prepare a bowl of fruit: chunks of cantaloupe, sliced pineapple, diced fresh strawberries. She poured orange juice over the fruit and placed the bowl in the refrigerator.

She glanced at her watch. It was almost nine-thirty, and at this rate they would never make it to church. She decided to wake her husband.

He was still lying in bed, the covers tucked around his chin.

"Don! Wake up! You planning on sleeping all day?"

He yawned, stretched his arms over his head, peered at her through half-shut eyes.

"God, I was so tired, honey, didn't even hear you come to bed." He reached for her hand. "I'll make it up to you, I swear."

"Must have been some week."

"It was a *busy* week," he allowed.

"Well, come on, shower and we'll eat. Breakfast is ready."

Leanne had always seen their marriage as a comfortable one, like a well-worn slipper. One's toes moved easily into the proper spaces and the result was ease and comfort.

She and Don worked as a team, jointly making important decisions. Raising their children, buying their first house, a new car for Leanne, investing their money. They worked together in every facet of their lives. They planned and enjoyed trips and outings with their two children. When the children went off on their individual pursuits, they began to take vacations, intimate cruises that made them feel like young lovers. It strengthened their marriage.

For their silver wedding anniversary, they had flown to Jamaica.

"Let's spend the money on ourselves," Don had suggested.

"Sounds good to me," she agreed. "Spend the money on us!" she laughed. "No one better to spend it on, right?"

"We come first, honey. It's always been you and me, babe! Always will be."

When they were first married they made love almost every night.

"Can't get enough of you. I'm so lucky to have you in my life," he frequently told her.

"I'm the lucky one," she would insist. "I will always love you, Don. Always."

Both felt secure in their marriage, and neither ever doubted that it would always remain so.

While shaving, Don peered into the mirror at his face and wondered, did his guilt show? He shivered as he rinsed the razor blade clean. How could he have been so weak? How could he have allowed such an awful thing to happen? As he thought about the past events, he realized he *had* become a willing participant. He did not have to go to Alisha's home, meet her parents, eat their food, let Alisha drive him back to the hotel. *Oh, God, Alisha*, he thought. *How can I keep her on my staff? What a mess!*

When he walked into the kitchen, warm, tantalizing aromas welcomed him. He was at home, where he wanted to be. He kissed his wife.

"Lee, it's so good to be home. I was straight out frazzled from that conference."

She patted his cheek.

"Glad you're home, Don. Been real lonely around here, 'specially with the children gone. Hope you're hungry."

"Oh, I am! Hotel food is all right, but nothing like home cooking."

He sat down at the kitchen table and Leanne handed him a chilled mimosa.

"Here's to us, Don," she said, touching her glass to his. "Here's to many more mimosas!" She took a few sips of her drink, smiling at him.

"Well, are you hungry?"

"You kidding me! Girl, I'm starved!" He picked up his knife and fork and playfully banged them on the table.

"Food, woman! Me want food!"

"Don, you're something else!" She laughed at his antics, her happiness flooding over her as she filled a plate for her husband. Beans, hash, bacon strips, and freshly sliced tomatoes on a lettuce leaf.

"Looks great, honey."

"Hot muffins and hot coffee coming right up."

"Hope you made enough for a hungry man."

"A dozen, but I don't think you can eat all of them."

"Want to see me try?" he asked, raising his eyebrows at her.

"God, no."

She prepared a plate for herself, joined him at the table. He looked at her plate and shook his head.

"Haven't got much on your plate."

"I know," she told him. "Gained a few pounds this week while you were away."

She broke open a warm muffin, ignored the butter on the table, and then took a sip of her coffee, which she always drank without cream or sugar.

"Don't lose too much. You look fine to me."

"That's because you've been away for a week. More coffee?"

She got up, went to the counter and returned with the carafe of hot coffee. She refilled his cup and added more to her own cup.

Playfully, he patted her on her backside as she returned to the counter.

"Better watch that," she chided, "not 'sposed to bother the help."

"But you're not the help . . . you're my wife, my dear woman."

She returned to her seat across from him. "I know, and don't you forget it," she teased. "Now, tell me about your week."

To get himself together after Leanne's last pronouncement, *God, she must never, ever know*, he drained his coffee cup and tried to look relaxed, although he felt like he was wearing a hairshirt, seeking redemption, although he did not feel worthy of forgiveness.

He replaced his empty cup in its saucer, pushed back from the table.

"It was busy, about three hundred conferees from all over the U.S., Canada, England and India."

"Meet any interesting people?" she wanted to know.

"Quite a few. Some with names I found it hard to pronounce."

"So, the focus of the conference?"

"Was stem cell research."

"That must have been interesting."

"It was, very. Don't know how much it will mean in my practice, dealing as I do with mainly chronic illness, but you never know."

He changed the subject, anxious not to continue.

"So," he said, "Janey is coming home today?"

"Sometime this afternoon. Bringing her roommate. They're driving. Don't know what her plans are, except she'll let us know when she gets here."

"Be glad to see her. You said Curtis was too busy to come this weekend."

"That's right. Some project he had to finish. Don, would you like a bowl of fresh fruit?"

"Perfect! You sit, I'll get it. In the fridge?"

"Bottom shelf, in a glass bowl."

As he retrieved the bowl of fruit, his guilt was almost suffocating. What a wonderful woman he had for a wife, and what a disastrous mess he had made of their lives.

He did not know how he could make love to his wife tonight as he had promised. And how was he going to face Alisha Monday morning at work?

"Thanks," Leanne said as he placed the fruit in front of her.

"You are more than welcome," he said, "more than welcome."

CHAPTER 13

A woman could not have been married for twenty-five years to one man without noticing whenever he was tense, out of sorts.

After Don's return from the medical conference that seemed to have tired him so much, she had noticed the change, but had not pressured him, knowing how much he always wanted to be a problem solver and that when he had solved the problem, he would then share it with her. There had never been secrets between them.

When Don returned to his office Monday morning, Becky Long, now promoted to secretary-receptionist, informed him that Alisha had called in, saying she needed a few days to recoup from her visit home, particularly since she learned of her mother's chronic illness. She planned to return on Thursday.

This piece of information disturbed Don. What did this mean? For him . . . and his future? What kind of message was she sending?

He went about his duties, anxious to know how things would go once Alisha returned to work. One thing he was certain about, this relationship could not continue. He was crazy to have allowed it to happen.

Thursday morning Alisha returned to work. Her fellow workers expressed sorrow over her mother's illness. Don added his sentiments as well.

Alisha smiled at him. "Thanks very much. It's good to know that people care."

He saw tears well up in her eyes.

"We all care, Alisha, you know that."

He was dismayed but not surprised when later that morning she joined him for coffee.

"We can't keep meeting like this," he whispered to her.

Wide-eyed, a blank look on her face, she answered, "Why not?"

"What do you mean, 'why not'?" he hissed.

"Nobody needs to know."

"I know! It's not right! I'm a married man!"

"We're not hurting anyone."

"Not hurting? Oh, yes, we are, and . . . I want you out of my office!"

"On what grounds? You know I'm indispensable."

He had never, ever seen this vindictive side of her. He lowered his head in his hands. "Just go!" His voice solemn and low. "Go! I'll give you two months severance pay. Just leave me *alone*."

He got up, his cup of coffee untouched, and stalked out of the cafeteria, his white medical coat flapping around his long legs.

A half hour later, having finished her coffee break, Alisha returned to the office. Just as she got to her station, the telephone rang. It was Becky Long. Now promoted to secretary, Becky had been training a new employee to take her place as a receptionist, and had, herself, been moved into her own office.

Alisha scowled when she answered the telephone and heard the summons. *Well, Don has wasted no time,* she thought. "I'll be right there," she said. Knowing that there was no love lost between Becky and herself, Alisha was determined to act in a matter-of-fact manner and not allow Becky to rattle her.

"Dr. Matthews asked me to have you sign these papers. He said he had spoken to you about your leaving . . . even without a two weeks' notice."

"Whatever," Alisha said taking the clipboard Becky handed her. There were several sheets to read, so she sat down in the chair facing Becky's desk.

"All you have to do is sign and date."

"I can read," Alisha snapped. More than that, she knew that under current law she could sue the medical association for wrongful discharge. But it was not Don's nurse she wanted to be. Her goal was to be his wife, if she followed her plans. Don Matthews, M.D., would be hers.

She was determined to take her time reading the material. Under Reasons for Termination of Employment, she read *Poor time and attendance,* which was, of course, not true, and *unacceptable professional conduct,* which Alisha figured was a matter of interpretation.

"Warned you," Becky said as she separated the papers from the clipboard, placing them in a folder that she sealed and filed in a cabinet behind her desk.

"We'll see, won't we?" Alisha snapped at the secretary as she took the severance pay handed to her.

When the last patient of the day left, Don called his staff into the conference room.

"Today," he told them, "we lost a colleague, but I'm certain each of you will carry on until we can get a replacement . . . which I hope will be soon. Thanks for your cooperation."

After Don's staff briefing about Alisha's leaving, everything seemed to be progressing nicely. It seemed as if she was barely missed as other nurses divided her caseload of patients between them.

Later that night in the condominium that she shared with her roommate, she laid out her plans. Wally's response was expected. "Girl, you are one crazy sister!"

"I'm crazy 'bout Don Matthews, and I'm goin' to get him anyway I can. And I need you to promise me that you'll keep this between us, okay? You promise?"

"I promise. Al, you're a grown woman. You're no dummy. But I could never deceive anyone like that."

"Thanks, sister-girl. I have to do this."

"Hope you've thought this out. But better be prepared. Down the road anything might upset the cart. You ready for that?"

"Ready, willing and able," was Alisha's response.

Alisha and Wally had met at the University of Massachusetts, Boston. They both were studying for advanced nursing degrees.

Cornwallis Farley, so named because her mother's maiden name was Cornwallis and she wanted her only child to carry the name of her Barbados ancestors.

Called Wally by friends, she and Alisha met at an alumni luncheon, renewed their friendship and ultimately bought a condo together.

Wally's degree was in Nursing Education and she taught at a college in the Boston area. Alisha's degree would have prepared her for nursing research, but she had not completed her dissertation on her study of sickle cell anemia, the disease which often affects people of color, or those of Mediterranean decent. This disease of misshapen red blood cells causes problems with the blood's circulation. Often, the clumping of these cells causes joint pain and blood clotting. Alisha's research dealt with new modalities for treatment. It bothered Alisha a great deal that she had not completed her work, but she vowed that when she finally married Don she could return to her study. A Ph.D. would enable her to bring even more to their marriage.

CHAPTER 14

When she met with Dr. Ames Baldwin, the owner of the sperm bank, he agreed with her that at age thirty she was at a good age to become a mother.

A fatherly figure, Alisha felt at ease with him as she explained her situation. "There's been no Mr. Right, and I do want to have a child. When Mr. Right does come along, he'll have to accept me and my child."

Dr. Baldwin was a board-certified fertility specialist. Alisha had found him in a medical directory. After her first appointment, she filled out the necessary papers and described the type of sperm donor she was seeking.

"He must be well-educated, a physician, scientist, lawyer, financier, engineer, and his age must be around thirty-five. I prefer he be of medium-brown complexion with smooth, regular features, tall and muscular like a tennis player, swimmer or baseball player. Not as muscular as a football or basketball player. And he should be healthy in mind and body," she added.

"Our donors are well screened, and we insist on a documented family history. I am sure, with our screening services, we will be able to meet your need. And I can recommend a physician who can perform the in vitro procedure for you. You'll need to have your ovaries checked for your egg supply and an optimum time during ovulation when you will receive your implantation."

"Oh, Curtis! Yes, I'm fine," Leanne said brightly, happy to hear her son's deep voice. She smiled as she held the telephone receiver to her ear.

"It's *so* like you, son, to think about me! I'm moving on. Had a meeting last week with the divorce mediation group and things are being taken care of. Both your father and I are satisfied."

"I should hope so, Ma. He owes you."

"I don't know about that. I just want what's fair to you kids."

"I don't want anything from the bastard . . ."

"Curtis," Leanne gently chided, "don't talk like that. You know your father loves you children. Always will. Wants to do right by you. He has said so more than once."

"Mom," Curtis' voice came over the phone in a quiet, somber tone, "Mom . . . I don't understand. I will never understand how *my* father . . ."

She insisted, "You don't have to understand. You have to accept it. We will probably never know what changed your father. I doubt even he knows. But you and I both know if your dad had an incurable illness we would still love him, want the best for him, right? Changes come into our lives and we must live with them or give up, and I don't want that for you. Or for any of us. For me, I've thought a lot about the change in your father . . ."

"Like what?" Curtis wanted to know.

"A midlife crisis. The sexual appeal of a younger woman to an older man."

"But, Ma, how can you still love him . . . and I know you do . . ."

"My dear," she said, "no matter what, I will always love your father until the day I die."

⟐

"New York? What a great idea, Don! Sure you can get away?"

Delighted to see the look of pure joy on his wife's face, Don hugged her. "Got it all planned," he said. "Marty is going to cover for any hospital patients, and I've cleared patient appointments for four days, giving the staff a long weekend. So all systems are go."

"Oh, Don, this is just wonderful. When do we leave?"

"I figure a Friday to Monday would be good. We'll take the shuttle from Green Airport on Friday, come back on Monday. I've been on line, have tickets for two Broadway productions. Not telling you which ones. Be a surprise!"

She kissed him. "You're the best husband a girl could have."

A frisson of guilt came over him as he saw the unmitigated love in her eyes.

"I try to be, Leanne, I try to be."

"Well, you *are*," she insisted.

Please, God, don't ever let her know.

The weekend in New York City was all that Don hoped it would be. As he had promised, Leanne was surprised and delighted when she found out that he had gotten tickets for *The Phantom of the Opera* for Friday evening, and on Saturday evening they had an early dinner in the hotel's dining room before taking a taxi to see *Cat on a Hot Tin Roof.*

"What a grand time we're having," Leanne said to Don as he helped her into the taxi to return to the New York hotel. "Don't know when I've had so much fun."

"That's what I want you to have, lots of fun, a real good time, you know," he said in a serious tone. "It's important that as a couple we spend quality time together . . . not to lose sight of the fact that we are together for life."

She glanced at him in the darkness of the cab's interior, saw the firm set of his jaw as he stared at the back of the cab driver's head. She knew he was serious, meant what he said, but she said nothing, merely reached over to squeeze his hand. He responded with a firm clasp of his own. *God, please, I can't lose this woman.*

When they reached the hotel he asked, "Would you like to stop in the lounge for a nightcap?"

"Don't think so. My feet are killing me in these heels. Maybe we can find something in the hotel fridge. I think I spied some bottles of wine . . ."

"That's what we'll do, then."

They moved, arm in arm, to the bank of elevators. As they rode to their room on the fourth floor, they talked about their children.

"I'd like to buy something new to wear for Curtis's graduation next month," she said as they left the elevator and walked to their room.

"That's a great idea," Don said, opening the door to their room. "I'm so proud of him. Jane, too. They haven't given us one bit of trouble. Curt did say he was taking the graduate exams for law school, didn't he?"

"Believe so. Think that's what he plans to do. He's hoping to get into Harvard Law School."

"Hope he makes it . . . have no doubts that he will. He's a smart kid."

Leanne heard the pride in her husband's voice about his only son, but she was quick to remind him, "Jane's a real treasure, too."

"Don't I know it," Don responded. "Our combined DNA did just fine. Agree?"

The next morning they went to one of New York's most famous shops as soon as the store opened. Leanne found what she liked, a white jacquard jacket with blue silk threads woven into it, fully lined with satin. She was able to find a pencil-slim navy crepe skirt that matched the jacket perfectly.

Don thought she should also buy new shoes. "Why don't we see if we can find a pair of navy pumps, or navy and white spectators . . . or are they out of style?"

Leanne disagreed, telling him, "Already have a pair of navy pumps that will do just fine. But," she added, "wouldn't mind having some new jewelry to go with this new outfit, if you're in the mood to spend money on me."

He gave her a wide grin. "My pleasure, my dear wife, my pleasure. I believe that 'Blue store,' Tiffany's, is not too far from here. Let's go have a look."

The well-groomed salesman who waited on them at the famous jewelry store could tell in a few moments that this man, this husband, was extremely anxious to please his wife. Having been in the business for more than thirty years, he recognized the spouse nervously intent on making amends.

After looking at many fine pieces of jewelry, Leanne finally selected a sapphire and pearl necklace with matching drop earrings and a single bracelet of the same stones.

As the salesman wrapped the jewelry into the famous blue Tiffany box, Leanne kissed her husband.

"Thanks, Don. I love you very much, thanks."

"I love you, Lea, and I want you to be happy, always."

"I know you do," she said softly.

As soon as they got back into their room Leanne kicked off her punishing shoes, threw her handbag on the bed, turned her back to her husband so that he could pull down the back zipper of the little black dress she had worn that evening.

She thanked him, saying, "I think a good soaking in the tub is what I need, Don. Do you want to use the bathroom before I do?"

"Go right ahead, hon, I'll see what's available for us here," he pointed to the room's small refrigerator. "You take your time, enjoy."

"It's been quite a day, what with shopping and everything."

"I know, Lea. I just wanted to please you . . . been a long time since we've been able to focus on ourselves."

"I know."

She stepped out of her dress, placed it on a hanger and put it in the closet. She retrieved her bathrobe and went into the bathroom.

The bathroom featured a Jacuzzi-like spa tub, and Leanne was determined to get the best therapy possible. When she settled into the tub, warm streams of jet-propelled water trained on her body made her relax and she felt the tensions of her work days at the real estate agency easing.

She thought about her husband, how eager he had been this weekend to please her, and for this weekend seemed to be the young eager Don she had fallen in love with so many years ago. *Time marches on, but our love only gets stronger. Thank you, God.*

When she finished bathing, she toweled herself dry, dusted some powder over her body, then put on the special nightgown that Don had not yet seen.

She went into the bedroom to find her husband dressed in his pajamas. He had turned the bed down and was placing a tray with wine, glasses, crackers and wedges of cheese down on the desk.

He gasped at the sight of her. "Oh, my God, Lea. Oh, my God! You're so beautiful!"

She raised her eyebrows.

"Think so?" she teased.

"Think so? I know so! God, you are as beautiful as you were on our wedding night . . . even more so! And you are mine, all mine."

He reached for her, pulled her close, the warm heat from her tantalizing clean body, the delicate fragrance from the powder she had dusted over her skin all made Don's fingers tingle as he ran his hands down from her face, neck and shoulders as he kissed her. She accepted his kiss with soft mewling sounds that only added to the extreme tension Don was feeling.

This was the woman he loved, the woman who gave him hope, and who loved him without reservations. This woman made no selfish demands on him, gave him only her best, took care of his needs before her own.

A fleeting image of Alisha floated in the back of his mind, but he quickly blocked it out, his focus on the wonderful woman he knew he would always love.

"Oh, Lea," he moaned against her throat as he picked her up, carried her to the bed. "Lea, I need you so much! Want you, need you. Please let me love you. Let's go back to our first night of magic."

Lying in the bed, she made no sound. He saw tears welling beneath her closed eyes.

Frantic, almost desperate, he practically tore off his pajamas and laid down beside her. "Don't cry, Lea, please don't cry."

She turned to face him. His mouth found hers and his hand smoothed over her warm, sleek, silk nightgown to caress the mounded breast beneath. Leanne responded by grasping her husband's head with both hands as their kisses deepened.

After twenty-five years of marriage, each knew the mating ritual that would bring them to fulfillment.

Words were no longer needed, only the sounds and moans of desire and deep pleasure.

Anxiety threatened Don. Would he fail his wife? The rising tension he felt was almost unbearable. He must not fail to meet the needs of his beloved Leanne.

With an agonizing groan, he pulled the interfering nightgown over her head. Immediately, his mouth sought to taste her breast, his tongue swirling over taut nipples. Lea responded to him as if it were the first time she had experienced this exquisite sensation. He felt her hips beneath him begin to move from side to side as she clutched his head to her breast.

Don's rock-hard body would not be denied as his mouth sought the favored areas of his wife's soft, pliant body. He was where he wanted to be, where he knew he was welcomed and wanted. He could not deny his heart's demands, and his body's reactions let him know it was useless to try.

CHAPTER 15

Sixty-five-year-old Nora Baskerville had been Don's patient since the death of her husband five years ago. Childless, the couple had been deeply devoted to each other, and the devastating change in her life and its associated loneliness and depression had eventually led to the onset of hypertension and type 2 diabetes. Weight gain due to comfort overeating was another of her problems. Today she was the doctor's last patient.

As the two left the examining room, Don told the widow he was pleased with how she was complying with the treatment plan he had designed. "I know it has not been easy, but you keep up the good work. And remember, diet and exercise will help keep your diabetes under control," he said reassuringly.

"Oh, my, yes, I'll do my best," she promised, giving him a bright smile. "And thanks, Dr. Matthews, for taking such good care of me."

"It is entirely my pleasure to do so," he said, gently patting her shoulder.

He returned to his office to make a few final notes on her computer file. Going into his private bathroom, he washed his face and hands before picking up his briefcase and grabbing his suit jacket from the clothes tree.

He had just reached the door to leave when his cell phone rang. He pulled it out of his briefcase, hoping it wasn't a crisis of some sort. He checked it. Alisha! He had not seen or heard from her in three months. What could she possibly want now?

"I must see you," she said when he called her.

"What for? What are you talking about? You *know* we're through seeing each other!"

"I know that. This is very important to both of us."

"What on earth are you talking about?"

"Like I said, this is *important!*"

Since their getaway weekend in New York City, Don and Leanne both recognized the exciting renewal in their relationship. It seemed to be as fresh and exciting as it was in the beginning of their life together. They were free to indulge one another, especially since both children were away at college. They could tease, frolic, play games, do whatever they wished, like carefree youngsters. These days, Don could hardly wait to get home to see what Leanne had planned. She enjoyed seeing the delight on his face when she would reveal her surprise.

He never knew what to expect when he arrived home, and after a day of meeting his patients' needs, he welcomed the various activities she had planned. Smiling to himself, he recalled the past Saturday. He had spent the afternoon at the barber shop and returned home about five that afternoon.

He found a note taped to the newel post of the front stairs.

"*Go up,*" was the message. Grinning with anticipation, he tore off the note and raced up the stairs.

"Lea, Lea, where are you?" There was no reply.

He went into their bedroom. He found another note taped to the mirror over the dresser, *You are freezing cold! Check the fireplace.*

On the fireplace mantelpiece was a large white card on which Leanne had printed in large block letters, *Not here, try the fridge.*

When he opened the refrigerator door, he found a box of frankfurters, a package of hamburger patties, a bowl of potato salad covered with cellophane, as well as a covered bowl of tossed green salad. There was also a platter of peeled shrimp with a container of cocktail sauce in the center.

Standing in the kitchen, staring into the opened refrigerator door, he detected the odor of burning charcoal. And that's when he found her, lounging in a deck chair out on the patio.

She laughed when she saw him standing in the kitchen door that led to the patio.

"Surprise! You're cooking tonight, Bubba! And your wife is hungry." She waggled a finger at him. "So, the fire is hot, let's get the show on the road."

"You little vixen!" He leaned over and kissed her. "May I please change into my chef's outfit?

"As long as you're quick about it."

He dashed off, loosening his tie as he did so. This was going to be a wonderful Saturday night.

He returned wearing tan shorts, a white tee shirt and his favorite Red Sox baseball cap. A dish towel was flung over his shoulder, and he was wearing a white chef's apron. He was carrying a tray with the food and supplies that he placed on a table beside the grill.

Leanne handed him a tall, frosted glass of lemonade.

"To keep you cool while you cook."

That Saturday night they remained out on the patio long after they had eaten. A full moon rose on the horizon, and when the evening breezes became chilly and the fire died out, they moved indoors, cleaned up and, arm-in-arm, went upstairs to bed.

They were in their night clothes, watching the late news.

"So, when are you going to tell the good doctor he is going to be a father?" Wally asked Alisha.

"Tomorrow," Alisha answered.

Wally yawned, stretched her arms over her head, then asked, "Tomorrow, where?"

"Actually, Wally, at his office at the medical center. Be after closing time. Hardly anyone there except the cleaning staff and maintenance people. Not too many professionals hang about after patient hours."

"Well, how are you going to get in? Didn't you have to turn in a key when you left?"

"Not before I had a duplicate made."

Wally shook her head.

"Girl, you are something else! How long has it been since you've seen him? There will be no doubt that when he sees that bump in your belly, he'll know you're pregnant."

"That's why I've kept my distance. It's been almost four months."

"Hope you know what you're doing, kid. I must say, you've got some chutzpah, as the Yiddish say."

"Wally, my dear friend, I know what I want and I won't stop until I get it!"

"What *do* you want?"

"I want what I should have . . . to be the wife of a prominent physician, enjoying his status and money. I want to be a whole lot more than the daughter of a steel mill worker from Pittsburgh! That's what I want, and I'm going to get it."

"But the man is married!"

"That's not my problem."

CHAPTER 16

Don hated lying to Leanne, but felt he had no other choice.

"Going to stop in at the hospital, Leanne," he told her with a hurried phone call. "Have to check on one of my patients. May not be home 'til maybe seven or so. Go ahead, eat without me."

He called the security desk in the lobby. "I'm expecting a patient around six. She used to work here as a nurse, Alisha Morton."

"Very well, Dr. Matthews. I'll ring you when she comes in and send her up."

It's not going to be very well, Don worried, pacing back and forth in his office from his desk to the office door and into his lavatory. God only knows what solace he could find there. Again to his desk to sit down, stare out of the window, but the view offered no comfort. His nerves were getting the best of him, palms were sweaty, he felt jumpy, and visions of impending doom clouded his mind.

If indeed Alisha is pregnant, she can sue me for child support. Oh, God, what a mess I'm in! Wasn't supposed to end like this! What was I thinking? You weren't!

He jumped when the telephone rang. "Ms. Morton is on her way up, Dr. Matthews."

"Thanks."

He went to his reception area to wait for Alisha's arrival. Almost immediately, it seemed to him, he heard a light tap on the door. He opened it. "Come in, Alisha. Let's move into my office."

He followed her as she walked ahead of him. He saw no sign of a pregnancy. She looked the same to him, just as he had last seen her almost four months ago. She was wearing black slacks and a loose black and white printed blouse. He thought she looked well.

"You're looking well, Alisha. How have you been?" He indicated a chair by his desk. She sat.

"I'm doing fine. You look very good yourself, Don."

"Thank you, but let's get on with this. Why is it so important for us to talk?"

He was standing beside his desk. She looked up at him.

"I think you should sit." She motioned to his chair. "I have some news that I think you should hear."

"News?"

"Well," she began slowly, twisting the handles of her Vera Bradley quilted handbag. "Don, I know it's been almost four months since we've been together, but I have to tell you that I am pregnant. You are going to be a father."

At hearing her fateful words, Don lowered his head in both hands. He said nothing.

Worried by his reaction, Alisha asked him, "Did you hear what I said?"

He shook his head in disbelief.

"I heard you, but it can't be true. I used protection."

"Not the last time at the motel."

He slapped his hand on his desk and glared at her, his voice rising in anger. "That damn motel! I should *never* have gone there! Damn! Are you sure?"

Wordlessly, she pulled up her blouse. He saw the tell-tale bump.

"See?" she said.

His face flushed, but his voice was as cold as ice. "Get rid of it."

"I can't. Not now."

"Why not?"

"I'm in my second trimester."

"You have to do something!"

"What? Why should I? This is your child! You knew I was a virgin. And I swear to God, I've never slept with any other man but you!"

She reached into her handbag for a tissue to wipe her tear-filled eyes.

"You *have* to marry me and do right by our child," she demanded.

"Alisha, I'm *already* married with two adult children . . ."

"That's your problem," she interrupted, "not mine, or our child's. He or she has a right to have a father."

"Do you know what you're asking me to do?"

"I can't help it! I love you, Don. You've got to know that." She starting to reach for him.

He pushed away in his chair, out of her reach. "Don't . . . don't touch me! You don't know what love is."

"Yes I do, I do! I truly love you, Don. You are the only man I've ever loved."

Don shook his head in denial, distraught with guilt, remorse, and stunned when in the back of his mind Mr. Morton's warning echoed, *Don't ever hurt my daughter,* and his promise, made with all sincerity, never to do so. Now this.

"This is a shock to me, Alisha, and you'd better go. I need to think. Go, please. Just go!"

He knew very well that she did not want to leave without some type of commitment from him, but his medical training had taught him *never to rush to judgment.*

"I'll get back to you."

"I'm living in a new condo," she told him. "Here's my card. Call me soon," and she added, "Please."

"I've got to consider my options."

"What do you mean, *options?*"

"Talk to my lawyer, for one thing. If this is truly my child . . ." His voice trailed off as the realization struck him.

"It is *your* child, and you know it!"

Again, tears welled up in her eyes, pleading for him to understand, to accept what she had told him. But denial was the truth he clung to. This situation could not be happening to him. *God, at fifty I'm too old to be a new father.*

Frank Jones greeted Don cordially when he appeared at the lawyer's office.

"Hi, Doc!" He extended a firm handshake to his friend. "How's it going?"

His observation of Don's haggard, hollow-eyed appearance made him question, "Looks like you haven't been sleeping well lately. What's up?"

Wearily Don accepted the chair that the lawyer indicated, sighed deeply, wiping his wet forehead with a limp white handkerchief he pulled from his trouser pocket.

"Man, as a matter of fact, haven't slept well for the past week."

"How can I help?"

"That's it, Frank. I don't know. I'm in a hell of a mess!"

"You! What's happened? Leanne? The kids?"

"No, no, they're fine."

"Well, what is it? A malpractice suit?"

"God, I wish to hell it was."

Frank heard the angst on his friend's voice and knew the man was in deep distress.

"Tell me, Don," he urged in a quiet tone of voice. "Start at the beginning."

Don found it impossible to look at his friend. With his right hand rubbing his forehead as if to mitigate his tale of woe, he spoke slowly.

"I . . . I met this girl . . ."

"No, Don, you didn't!"

"I did. I . . . we, had a couple of dates. I knew it was wrong, but this girl . . . Frank, I'm happy in my marriage to Leanne, believe me. But this . . . well, she was a nurse in my office. She's not a girl, she's thirty. Frank, I swear I didn't know it would come to this . . ."

"She's pregnant," Frank interrupted.

Don's face flushed, shame written all over it as he nodded in acknowledgment.

"Now, what does she want from you?"

"Marriage. She wants me to divorce Leanne and marry her! Frank, I never expected this. The effect she had on me, the sex . . . I was so attracted, I felt like a young stud. I've never experienced anything like it!"

The lawyer leaned back in his chair, his hands formed in a steeple pattern before his face. For a few moments he made no comment.

Then, reaching into his desk drawer, he pulled out a legal pad and a pen.

"She knows that you are married?'

"Says it's my problem."

"Right, and she wants you to divorce Leanne and marry her?"

"Yes."

"Do you want to? Divorce Leanne?"

"No, no, no! My God, Frank, no!"

"How do you know it's your child?"

"She was a virgin."

Frank Jones said, "That's what she told you and . . . you believed her?"

"Wasn't thinking, Frank, just responding to the moment."

"You know," the lawyer said, "even if you don't marry the girl, the bastardy law makes her able to demand child support for the child's welfare. Case law," he added, "that is to say common law, stipulates that."

"God, Frank, I'm doomed."

"Not yet. We'll see what we can do. For one thing, if you do consider marriage, you might insist on a pre-nuptial agreement."

"I'm not sure I *want* to marry her. How can a marriage be only about sex? So far, that's all we share."

"You forget the child."

"I can hardly put my mind around having a child. My God, I'll be an old man by the time he or she starts driving a car!"

"Another thing," Frank said, "you've got to provide for your other children, too."

"I know that. And Leanne as well."

"Right. She may want alimony. After all, *you* are the offender in this situation."

"Don't I know that."

"Then you have to consider your pension plan, any annuities, IRA—how those options are to be evaluated and considered."

"And, Frank, my practice . . ."

"Well, that's a valuable asset, too, that has to be considered. How much money you can expect to earn before retirement. Now," Frank tore off the top sheet of the legal pad, "I would advise you to continue to pay for your children's education."

"Curtis graduates this year, and Jane will be in her third year."

"Seeing that Curtis is over twenty-one, your legal responsibility for him has ended. Jane you may want to see finish school even though she is an adult, over eighteen."

"Frank, I feel trapped, looking for a way out. I don't love Alisha, but I feel that I owe her *and* the child. Especially the child. Don't think it's a good basis for marriage, but . . . I see no alternative. Leanne won't *want* me when she finds out that I have been unfaithful, and . . . I can't blame her."

"So, when are you going to tell her?"

"Tonight. I've made arrangements to move into the residents' quarters at the hospital until I can find an apartment."

"It's just as well that you tell her soon. She'll need her own lawyer, so tell her that I will be happy to meet with her and her lawyer anytime that's convenient. All together we'll try to sort this out to everyone's satisfaction."

"Frank," Don asked, "if Leanne agrees to the divorce, how long will it take? Alisha wants us to marry before the child . . ."

"That may be what she wants, but she may not be able to insist on it. The courts have their own calendars, but we'll see."

CHAPTER 17

Don was awarded a final decree of divorce, with the various lawyers' combined efforts that disposed of all matters of contention between Leanne and Don, and he became free to marry Alisha. She did not know when that would take place. The lawyers had arranged it so that it was not necessary for Don or Leanne to appear in court, since the divorce had been agreed upon.

She had told Alan Spencer, "I cannot look at Don without having bitter thoughts about his unfaithfulness. Never in my life did I think he would betray me."

"Your feeling is understandable, Leanne. And because we have settled all the contingencies, the sale of the house, the trust fund for each child, the Cape house deeded to you, your refusal of alimony . . . but you will be able to make such a request if . . ."

"No, Alan, I don't want any money from him, only that he pay for the children's education and a trust fund for each one when they reach twenty-five. I'm able to support myself. And with the sale of our house," her voice quavered, "I . . . I expect to be able to buy a three-bedroom, two-bath home so that the children have a place to call home."

"You'll let me know when everything is over? I expect to be at the Cape." She reached into her handbag and gave him her card. "Thank you, Alan, for everything. Your mediation group worked so hard to help me get through these uncharted waters."

"Leanne, it was our pleasure, believe me." He walked her to the door of his office, shaking her hand.

"Stay well, and call if you need me for anything."

Since the children were away, Curtis studying for the LSAT exam, living in an apartment in Roxbury, and Jane now a junior at Simmons College, Leanne was glad that they were continuing with their own lives. She was proud of them, even though Curtis could hardly manage his anger at his father.

"He's not worth calling a father!" he declared to his mother. On the other hand, Jane mourned for her father as if he were dead.

❧

Six months after the divorce was final, Alisha insisted that the wedding take place in Pittsburgh. Although her mother's mental state had not changed, she seemed to understand that her daughter was getting married and that she would soon become a grandmother.

Frank Jones agreed to be Don's best man, and Alisha's lifelong friend, Julie Donner, was her maid of honor.

Mr. Morton was not too happy over what he thought was a "shotgun" wedding. Nonetheless, he approved of Don "doing right" by his only child.

"I'm right glad that you are a man of honor," he told Don.

"I always try to be, sir," Don told him.

Everyone was on the patio, waiting for the service to begin. About six of the older couple's closest relatives were there, seated before a table with an array of flowers on it.

The officiating minister, a Rev. Otis Evans, came onto the patio, Bible in hand. Mr. Morton introduced Don, then said, "I'm going to get Alisha, and we can start the ceremony."

When Alisha walked through the patio doors on her father's arm, Don gasped. She looked lovely. Her pixie-like dark hair was covered with a pearl seeded cap and she wore a white satin suit with an A-line skirt that fell to her knees. The jacket crossed over the front and was anchored on the left side with one large gold button. She wore white sandals and carried a bouquet of roses and baby's breath.

After the brief ceremony, the wedding party and guests moved into the dining room, where Mrs. Morton's church ladies served a meal of roast beef, gravy, peas and rice, string beans, salad, coffee, and slices of a small wedding cake.

Frank offered a champagne toast and Don rose from his seat to thank everyone for coming and for their good wishes. He toasted his smiling bride and kissed her, to the delight of all, especially the bride.

Don had explained to Alisha that because of her advancing pregnancy, he decided they would drive back to Boston.

Becky had been planning with her husband, John, to vacation at their time-share condo in Aruba. She was very surprised when it turned out to be the week of Don's wedding.

Already there was a certain amount of tension in the office with the startling news of the doctor's divorce and impending marriage to Alisha Morton, their former colleague.

Becky herself was concerned when the doctor had gathered them all together in the conference room and told them of the changes in his life.

"I'm closing my office for the last week of this month. I'm getting married, and because I'll be away, you will each have a paid vacation for that week."

There were murmurs of shock and dismay, with comments ranging from "No need to pay us," to "Hope all goes well," to "Good luck."

Becky saw tears glistening in the doctor's eyes as he accepted hugs and good wishes from his staff. She was the last to leave and told Don, "You did not have to give paid vacations, Dr. Matthews."

"I wanted to, Becky. I wanted to."

For Becky the whole situation was worse because her fears had come true. She had recognized Alisha Morton's manipulative behavior and was not surprised when she heard the news. She wished now that she had warned her boss, but how does one tell the boss what to do and whom to see? As a mere secretary you *don't,* not to a board-certified internist who is responsible for the health and welfare of hundreds of patients.

She and John had honeymooned in Aruba and subsequently bought a time-share condominium on Palm Beach on the west coast of the island. The island's soft, alluring winds, white sandy beaches, made it a favorite destination for them.

For herself, Becky looked forward to having quality time with her husband of ten years. Despite her deep concern for her boss, she determined that her first priority was to her husband and herself. However, she did discuss the doctor's situation with John a few days before their departure.

"John?"

"Yes, what's on your mind?" Her husband put down the newspaper he had been reading.

Becky had brought a laundry basket of clothes into the family room and was folding towels, sheets, shirts, socks and other assorted articles of clothing into piles.

"Tell me, John, how can a man like Donovan Matthews become so beguiled by a selfish, worthless woman that he can throw away his wife of twenty-five years as easily as changing his clothes from a business suit to . . . to sweatpants?"

"Don't think it's as easy as that, my dear."

"It must be," Becky protested, "or how could he do it? I knew Alisha was out to get him, but couldn't *he* see that?"

As a certified public accountant and an auditor for the Internal Revenue Service, John dealt in reality, factual realities like tax laws and numbers. From his pragmatic, practical viewpoint, he tried to help his wife understand.

"To answer your question, Becky dear, she 'put out,' was a temptress, and your doctor responded. It's all very simple . . . the woman offers and the man accepts. It's in his nature to do so."

"I don't believe that!"

"Believe it. It is the way males and females were constructed. Sex always wins over the brain. If it were not for sex, none of us would be here."

He raised his eyebrows at his wife.

"Well, maybe, since you put it like that. But it still seems to me that a well-educated, medically trained person would not be so easily affected by raging hormones, like some teenager."

"Look, Becky." Her husband folded his newspaper and placed it on the table beside his chair. He spoke to her in a serious tone. "I'm not a doctor, but I do remember there was this guy who said the women were driving him *crazy*. He could not deal with it. His folks had to come and take him home. He was eventually admitted to a psychiatric facility . . . was there for years, I heard."

"*Women* did that to him?"

"Evidently he couldn't cope with the pressure so many females put on him. To meet the sexual demands of so many was more than he could take. It was easier to withdraw from real life and enter one in which he did not have to deal with the overwhelming, debilitating problem. Insanity was his defense mechanism."

CHAPTER 18

Cornwallis Farley went out onto the balcony of her condo, which faced the beach. The ocean was a sparkling blue and the soft white sand beckoned to her, but she had work to do.

She was leaving the island the next morning and had yet to pack her bags. With a cup of morning coffee in her hand, she sat, taking a last look at the beautiful scene.

Relaxing in a comfortable lounge chair, she became aware of some movement on the balcony adjacent to hers. Looking over, she saw a brown-skinned young but matronly woman with a cup of coffee in one hand and a book in the other.

"Hello," she said.

"Oh, hi," Becky answered. "Didn't see you at first."

"Did you just get in?"

"Yes, last night. My husband and I arrived about nine. Hope we didn't disturb you."

"Not at all."

Reaching across the divide, Wally offered her hand.

"I'm Cornwallis Farley. Most people call me Wally."

"I'm Becky Long."

After shaking hands with her new neighbor, Becky turned to the sliding door to the apartment.

"John, come out and meet our neighbor."

Her husband came out smiling as Becky introduced him to Wally.

"Nice to meet you, ma'am. Where are you from?"

"Please, call me Wally. Boston, I'm from Boston."

"So are we! Imagine that! Where do you live in Boston?"

"I'm up near Mass General Hospital. I'm a nurse educator."

John smiled. "Must be nice, a short commute."

"You bet! And you, where do you folks live?"

"We live in Milton. I work for the Internal Revenue Service." He waved his hand at Becky. "She's a secretary to a very fine internist."

Becky added, "As a matter of fact, he's getting married this week, so he closed down the office and the staff all received a week's paid vacation."

"What kind of physician did you say he was?" Wally asked.

"He's an internist, a wonderful doctor. All of his patients love him. Donovan Matthews. Maybe you've heard of him?"

"Don't think so. If he had staff privileges at MGH, I might . . ."

"I believe most of his patients go to Beth Israel."

"Still a small world, isn't it?" Wally said. "Now I'm sorry I'm leaving in the morning. We could have spent more time together . . . might well know some of the same folks."

"Let's hope we see each other again," Becky said.

"That would be nice. Well, I've got to pack. I hope you both enjoy your holiday."

Wally went into her apartment, reflecting on what she had just learned.

So Alisha Morton has had her way, marrying Donovan Matthews.

A fierce argument had erupted between the two roommates when Wally finally had to make it clear that she did not approve of Alisha's plans.

"You know, Alisha, your deceit in this relationship may someday come back to haunt you. You can't expect to build a good life on lies."

Bristling, Alisha fired back, "Look, this is my life, and I know what I want, and I'll do whatever I need to do to get it! I will not be denied. Don Matthews doesn't even have an inkling of how happy I will make him, especially after I have *our* child."

Wally had risen from her seat in the living room and headed toward the door to her own room down the hall.

"Still don't know how you can be such a dishonest person . . . to trick an innocent man . . . don't see how you can live with yourself."

Alisha flipped her hand under her chin at her roommate.

"Very well, my friend, very well. Don is an extremely successful practitioner, and I plan to be living the good life as the wife of a doctor."

"But to *lie* to him, make him think . . ."

Before she could finish her sentence Alisha snapped, "You promised!" she spat out the words. "You promised!"

"And," Wally said firmly before she walked out of the room, "I'll keep my promise. *Lying* has never been *my* style."

She went into her own room and made a call to the real estate agent who had sold them the condo. She had to find another place to live.

Alisha was nervously curious. Don had promised her an extraordinary honeymoon. He had told her, "I've closed my office for the week for us to spend together."

"Oh, where are we going?"

"It's a surprise. I think you'll like it. At least I hope you will."

"I know I will!"

"Good, looking forward to it."

"I can't wait. Will I need special clothes?"

"Don't think so, but if you do, we'll buy them."

"Don, I love you so much! You're wonderful!"

"I try to do my best."

"Oh, I know that. Never doubted that," she said.

Sitting in the front seat of the car, she snuggled up to him to get as close as possible and squeezed his arm. "I'm so happy."

"I'm glad," he said, hoping he sounded that way.

He looked over at her. She seemed to be glowing with good health, seemed happy and relaxed being with him. He felt as if he were on a new adventure . . . perhaps this situation might work after all. Indeed, he knew he enjoyed sleeping with her. He rather hoped the relationship might be better after the baby came. Suddenly his ego knew no bounds at the thought of the pleasure he derived from being with her. As much as he missed his family, and he did, he was energized by the fact that at fifty he was able to father a child. He could hardly wait. Even with the new technologies in medicine, he knew that there were men in their sixties able to produce healthy children.

He was extremely proud of himself, though he had not expected this outcome. His ego strengthened, he was excited about this new life.

He sensed that Alisha was tiring. They had been on the Pennsylvania Turnpike for about four hours since leaving Pittsburgh.

"Are you all right?" he asked.

"Doing just fine," she said. "Might have to make a pit stop down the road, though."

"Bladder getting full?"

"Well, yes, as a matter of fact."

"Let me check the GPS and see if we can find the nearest facility for an overnight's stay. Are you with me on this?"

She rewarded him with a smile.

"Absolutely!"

But disappointment nagged at her. It was apparent that there was not going to be an exotic cruise, a trip to Europe or Hawaii. Don was heading back to Boston.

CHAPTER 19

Gloria Clark kept close watch over Leanne, who had been commuting from the Cape to her office. The strain was beginning to show. Losing weight, dark circles under her eyes, and Gloria could not count the number of times that she heard Leanne exhale long, drawn-out sighs. She could tell that her friend was suffering, and she wanted to help her if she could. The opportunity came sooner than she expected.

The next morning when Leanne drove in from the Cape, Gloria greeted her with an excited smile.

"Leanne, this listing just came in! I think it's what you're looking for."

Leanne took a seat beside Gloria's desk. Putting on her reading glasses, she said, "Let me see."

The listing read, *Cape house, three bedrooms, two baths, large family room, new kitchen with up-to-date appliances, granite countertops, ceramic tile, hardwood floors, finished basement w/ two-car garage. Fully landscaped 1 acre lot.*

"It sounds like something I might want to look at, Gloria."

"Good. I've already called the agent. She will meet us there at ten."

"Sounds okay to me. Let me get a cup of coffee and catch my breath and then we'll go."

"And Leanne, guess what? It's not far from your old neighborhood. It's about five or six streets away. You may even recognize it when you see it. The seller's name is Griffin . . ."

"I *know* that house, Gloria. A Mr. and Mrs. Archer Griffin . . ." Leanne interrupted Gloria. "The Griffin children went to high school with my two kids. I've been inside once or twice. As I recall, it was fairly nice, but they may have made changes to it."

"It would be nice if you could find a house you're somewhat familiar with. Make it easier for you to make the adjustment to a new place."

"That's true. There's been quite enough of an upheaval in my life," Leanne sighed.

She finished her coffee and picked up her purse and car keys.

"Well, let's go see what there is to see. I really want to have a home for the children to come home to, whenever they choose. I hate the idea of this divorce disrupting their lives."

"I know you do. I understand perfectly. Well, let's have good vibes! 'Nothing beats a trial but a failure,' my mother always said."

By the time Don and Alisha reached a motel with a vacancy sign on the turnpike, both were bone tired. Don from driving almost five hours, and Alisha, angry and disappointed when she learned Don's plans for their honeymoon.

"Why are we on this turnpike, Don?" she had asked. He heard the anger in her voice but realized he had to tell her the truth. So he answered her question.

"I'm sorry, Alisha, but the truth of the matter is the divorce and our marriage have cost me plenty. We will have to be thrifty until I can recoup some of the money I had to spend. I'm sure you understand . . ."

"Oh, I do, I do!" But the frown on her face told him otherwise.

Indeed, she was very angry, but she knew that now was not the time to reveal her true feelings. She dared not let him know that she had learned from a former colleague of Don's magnanimous gesture in giving his staff a paid vacation. That, in itself, would surely have paid for the overseas honeymoon she wanted.

The motel they finally chose was one of a large chain. The parking facilities were adequate, attractive, and the well-maintained landscaping lessened her disappointment a little. She decided to get all she could out of it, use all the amenities she could.

As soon as the bellhop had shown them to their room, Don tipped him, turning to Alisha, who was sitting in one of the armchairs. He said, "Look, hon, it's been quite a day for both of us. I'll order up something for us to eat, so why don't you relax. I'll draw a bath for you that'll make some of the weariness go away."

"I guess so . . ." Her voice trailed off in her attempt to garner more sympathy from him.

He wagged his finger at her. "Now, none of that!" he said and smiled. "These are doctor's orders. Now, what would you like to have for your supper?"

"Since I'm 'eating for two,'" she reminded him, "I'd like a sirloin steak, medium rare, a small baked potato, garden salad with ranch dressing, and fat-free milk."

"That sounds good. I'll order the same, except I'll have coffee. Should be here by the time your bath is done."

As Alisha slid into the tub of warm water that Don had prepared for her, she realized that she would have to make some serious behavior adjustments to maintain her husband's loyalty. She had to avoid any slipups and focus on him, be sure to meet *his* needs.

Her sexual talents were what she had used to snare him, and she was bound and determined to use all skills necessary to keep him enthralled with her. Using any wiles she could dream up, she intended to bind him ever closer to her. And, she decided, she would begin tonight. She would be as attractive to him tonight as she was before her pregnancy began.

Swirling the warm, scented water around her abdomen, she promised her baby, "Your turn will come later. Don't you worry, Mommy's going to see to that."

CHAPTER 20

They had reached the Massachusetts Pike when Alisha finally questioned her husband.

"Don, where are *we* going to live? You know my roommate and I have put our condominium up for sale. I do have some furniture in storage that maybe we can use, but . . ."

"I know you are anxious to know, Alisha, and I hope you'll be pleased when we do get *home*."

"So," she prodded, "*where* is home?"

"It's a brand new house, built on what was once a naval air station."

"A *new* house? Oh, Don, I forgive you for not taking me on a honeymoon! A new house, never been lived in, brand spanking new?"

Her joyous excitement pleased him. He was glad that she was so happy. He hoped that becoming involved in the new house would keep her occupied. Don hated to admit, even to himself, that the increased sexual activity Alisha wanted was beginning to wear him down.

She cried, sobbing in his arms. "You don't want to love me because I'm fat and . . . pregnant! Don, you know you made me this way! Now I'm no longer attractive to you?"

With Leanne it had been like a soft-shoe dance. But with Alisha it was like a rip-roaring, hard-stepping tap dance. Even he noticed his racing heartbeat and breathless pants.

He had also felt the baby's movements and had used a borrowed fetoscope from a colleague to check the baby's heartbeat. In doing so, he discovered the baby was lying in a transverse position in the uterus. He said nothing to Alisha, but did call her obstetrician.

"Don't mean to be a fuddy-duddy," he told him, "but I noticed that Alisha's baby is lying in a transverse position."

"Oh, yes, Don, I'm aware of that. As you know, babies often change positions in utero, almost like bobbing up and down, changing positions. And quite often they will get into the head down position just before delivery . . . and at times we are able to manipulate them into the right position."

"I see."

"Not to worry, Don. And if we have to do a C-section, we will. But we'll worry about that when the time comes. So far, everything is fine."

Don exhaled. "Glad to hear that, Joe. And I know we are all safe in your very capable hands. Thank you."

"No problem," his friend replied.

He said nothing of his concern to Alisha, but was quietly relieved when she began to slow down on her sexual demands.

Soon, however, another pressing issue came to his attention. One Monday morning, soon after his telephone conversation with Alisha's doctor, Becky Long tapped on his office door a few minutes before he was to see his scheduled patient.

"Yes, Becky, what can I do for you?"

Immediately noticing the sober look on her face, he offered her a chair. She sat down, a brown folder in her hand. Her sober look alerted him.

"What is it, Becky?"

"I'm very sorry, sir, but . . ."

"Becky, I've never seen you so upset!"

She handed him a folder. "These came in over the weekend."

He took the folder from her, opened it and began to read several e-mails.

Sorry, I have gone to another doctor. I can't believe in a doctor who commits adultery. I will no longer be your patient. I trusted you, Dr. Matthews, but my trust is gone.

He looked at Becky as more than a dozen e-mails and letters fell from his grasp.

"What? What's happening?" His eyes widened, his face flushed, he stared at his secretary.

"How many?"

"Sorry, doctor. About twenty so far. Even Mrs. Baskerville and Mr. Alexander, two of your most faithful . . ."

"I know, I know. But, Becky, I didn't expect this kind of reaction. My personal life should have nothing to do with my professional ability . . ."

"I agree, but you must consider your clientele. African-Americans are usually deeply grounded in their religious beliefs, particularly the senior citizens we most often see."

"I recognize that, but to make judgments on personal matters, not professional . . ."

"I know, I know, and I'm sorry. What are you going to do?"

"I don't know, Becky. I don't really know."

Leaving the office, she told him that his first patient had arrived.

"Give me a few minutes, Becky. I'll be right along."

With his head in his hands, Don worried about his future. True, many of his patients attended the same church. He himself had attended St. Barnabas with his former wife and children. Some of his patients worshipped there, too. But now that he was married to Alisha, he no longer worshipped at the Episcopal church.

He placed the troubling file in a lower drawer of his desk and went into his lavatory to wash his hands. He then went out to the first examining room door, selected the patient's file and with a forced cheerful smile greeted his first patient of the day.

"Hello, Mr. Grant," he said, shaking the patient's hand.

Don was a physician, had always put his patients first. And on that Monday morning, despite his worries, he determined to do just that for this next patient. He opened the patient's chart.

Leanne bought the Griffin house, and both Curtis and Jane were happy with their new home. Jane was happy at the idea of a new room that she could decorate any way she wanted.

Curtis told his mother that he certainly did not miss their old house, and since there were no reminders of his father, the new house was just fine with him.

His mother chastised him. "Curtis, remember, he is your father. The only one you'll ever have. Don't allow yourself to be bitter. If you do, it will take away who you are . . . and I don't want that. I want only good things for you and Jane. And despite what's happened, I know your father does, too."

Curtis walked away from his mother, grumbling something under his breath, but Leanne said nothing more. She knew exactly how her son felt. She felt the same heartbreaking betrayal, but knew that if she focused on that, her life would be ruined, and she was determined not let that happen.

The house had all that she wanted. It was well-constructed, passed the inspection easily, and other than changing the paint color in the bedrooms, it had been "move-in" ready.

She was happy with the crown moldings in the living and dining rooms. The kitchen, as stated in the listing, was very well-appointed. Even Jane had decided that maybe she would try her hand at cooking.

"Be my guest," her mother said when she saw, to her relieved delight, that her daughter was happy.

Leanne knew that both of her children loved and missed their father, but she hoped the new house would help them to move on to successful lives.

CHAPTER 21

Don and Alisha had settled into a somewhat reasonably comfortable relationship. It was no longer "bells and whistles," and Alisha was entering into a nesting mode in her pregnancy. She went shopping for baby clothing, baby bath articles. For the crib, she and Don shopped for sheets and blankets.

Don was glad that she was involved in this activity, and relieved that she seldom asked about *his* day. He did not want to tell her about his declining practice, hoping that the worst was behind him. However, when one of his nurses left on maternity leave, he did not replace her, making no explanation to the remaining staff. Becky had assumed the role of nurse manager, running the office quite smoothly. He realized that she had become his most valuable employee.

He told her, "Becky, you have been a godsend to me and I intend to raise your salary just as soon as things stabilize around here."

"No need for that," she said. "I'm happy that you are pleased."

"Well, I want you to know this office could not run without your expert help. I will *never, ever* be able to forget your loyalty and help."

In the weeks leading up to her due date, Alisha began to complain to Don about her discomfort. She felt that she was unattractive to him despite his attempts to reassure her otherwise. However, he found himself comparing her with his former wife. Leanne had been joyous and excited during her pregnancies, and accepted discomfort as part of the eventful process. At every new change in her body, she would say to Don, "Look what our love has done! We're creating a new person not like anyone else on earth, Don!"

He would try to temper her excitement with practical responses such as, "It's nothing new. Been happening for millions of years."

"It's the first time for us," she said before Curtis was born. "Should be in the headlines, *A STAR IS BORN.*"

"You're nuts, you know that, Lea? But you're *my* nutty wife, and I love you."

As he tried to see to Alisha's many needs and tried to block out her irritating sighs and moans, he conceded that he was not being fair to Alisha. Curtis had been born twenty-three years ago, when he was twenty-seven, just out of medical school and beginning a new career.

At fifty, he worried about so many things, his dwindling practice, trying to furnish the new split-level house he shared with Alisha, who appeared to have little interest in it, although she said she would start to do so once their child was born.

His whining wife made him long for the serenity of his former wife. He truly hoped things would improve once the baby was born. All he wanted was a healthy child.

He attended the birthing classes with her and was pleasantly surprised to find that he was not the oldest expectant father. He met one or two men helping their wives learn proper breathing techniques during contractions, how to work through their contractions to make the process easier.

He noticed that Alisha was less than enthusiastic about the coming birth, which surprised him, knowing that as a professional nurse she should understand the birthing procedure and become more involved. To him she seemed to have taken the role of bystander, watching, not participating. He began to wonder as he saw her lack of excitement over the coming event if she could be predisposed to be a victim of a post-partum depression. He recognized her behavior as troubling, but hoped it would improve when the baby came.

On a hot, humid August night at one-thirty in the morning, Don was awakened by Alisha's moans. He turned on the bedside lamp.

"What's wrong?"

One look at her contorted face gave him an answer.

"You're having a contraction?"

She nodded, too frightened to speak, her eyes begging him for help.

He got out of bed and dressed quickly in slacks and a tee shirt, all the while keeping a watchful eye on his wife.

She gasped as another contraction moved over her extended abdomen. Don placed his hand over her belly to time the internal struggle.

"Seems you are going into active labor," he told her. "I'm going to call Joe Collins, tell him what's going on."

He did so, snapping his cell phone shut, placing it in his pants pocket.

"He's going to meet us at the hospital. Here's your bathrobe," he told her, "and your slippers. I'll get your bag out of the closet."

By the time they reached the car in the driveway, Alisha had another strong contraction which made her cry out.

"Don, help me!"

"Take deep breaths. Breathe through the pain . . ."

"I can't, I can't. I don't . . . don't want to have a baby! Help me, Don, help me-e-e!"

Her reaction startled Don, and he prayed silently that they would get to the hospital in time. Because it was early morning, the traffic was light and he hoped for the best.

Alisha lay back against the passenger seat, her hands across her abdomen, her eyes closed, her mouth in a rictus grin as if she could will the pain away.

He knew she was afraid, and as he drove through the velvet black night he felt sorry for her, but only she could do the work of bringing their child into the world. Only she would feel the labor pains.

Sighing deeply, she asked him, "Is this going to take long?"

Wanting to reassure her, he knew he had to be truthful.

"Alisha, I don't know. It could be hours or it could be soon. Depends on how quickly your cervix dilates. Joe will be able to tell you once he examines you. And I will be right by your side. I know you will do fine."

"I—I . . . hope so. Didn't know it would be this hard."

"You're a trooper, Alisha. A real trooper. Trust me."

Pulling into the hospital parking lot, he remembered he had said those same words to Leanne . . . twenty-three years ago when Curtis had been born.

CHAPTER 22

The day Wally severed her relationship with Alisha, she couldn't have been more certain that she had made the right decision. She'd had a strenuous day of teaching nurses, many of whom were registered nurses who had passed the national exams and thought there was nothing more they needed to learn. She had been tired and irritable, as she knew most of her students were in her class for the sole purpose of qualifying for the higher salaries an advanced degree would give them.

Wally had become increasingly disapproving of Alisha's outrageous deceit and extremely uncomfortable with her own knowledge of it. She *had* to remove herself from what she felt was an untenable position. She no longer felt kindly toward her friend; indeed, she was feeling just the opposite. It was imperative that she move—and it couldn't be soon enough.

When she arrived at the condo later that afternoon, Alisha was on the living room couch, a bag of potato chips and a cold drink on the coffee table in front of her.

"Hi," she said, picking up her drink to take a swallow. Her bland, unconcerned expression infuriated Wally.

"Hi, yourself!" she said, plopping down on a chair across from Alisha. Then, after a few moments of uncomfortable silence, she blurted, "Look, I'm outta here!"

"What? You're leaving? How come?"

"Why are you asking me that, Alisha? You know dog-gone well that I don't approve of what you're doin'. Either I buy you out of this mortgage or you buy me out, but I'm *not* staying!"

In a calm, matter-of-fact voice, Alisha responded, "Why don't we both sell? We bought together, we can sell together."

A suddenly relieved Wally said, "Fine, if that's all right with you. I've already lined up an agent, so why don't we let her put the place on the market, see what happens."

"Okay by me," Alisha said, munching on a potato chip.

Alisha's devil-may-care attitude was becoming almost impossible for Wally to tolerate, but she held back her anger and described the plans she had already made.

"I've rented an apartment on Charles Street, near the hospital. As soon as I move and get settled, I'll let you know."

"Good. I'll be leaving, too, as soon as Don and I set a date."

"So you think it will be a good idea, keep up our payments and let our real estate agent handle everything?"

"What kind of price should we be asking?" Alisha said.

Wally told her she thought the agent with her knowledge of the current market might be able to help them with that.

Alisha agreed, adding, "Until it's sold we will each keep up with our mortgage payments, like we said, until then."

"That's right, and if we move out soon, new owners can move in at their pleasure."

"Makes sense, Wally."

Wally was pleased that Alisha was behaving in a calm, rational manner; she knew all too well how angry Alisha could be whenever she did not get her way. She decided to take advantage of her roommate's good humor and reveal the rest of her plans.

"I'll be out of here by this weekend, into my new apartment, and then I'm off on vacation."

"Good for you. Where you going?"

"Taking a cruise to Alaska. I've always wanted to see the glaciers, the Cascade Mountains and some of the national parks. I really do need a change, looking forward to it. By the way, the real estate agent's name is Mrs. Sharlene Prior. Here's her card. I think you'll like her."

"As long as she can help us sell this place . . ."

Mrs. Prior had found a buyer for the condo, and by the end of the month papers had been passed between the buyers and sellers.

Wally and Alisha shook hands with the new owners, a newly married couple anxious to start married life with a home of their own.

Then Alisha and Wally shook hands with Mrs. Prior. After it was over, they shared a brief hug, each knowing that the relationship was over.

For Wally, it was as if a weight had been lifted from her shoulders now that she was no longer living with Alisha. But the deceitful knowledge that she still shared bothered her. What could she do? She'd sworn to keep Alisha's action a secret.

Living apart from Alisha, she began to focus on her new apartment and her own life, realizing that she had no investment or responsibility in her roommate's life, or indeed her future. She set about making plans for her Alaska adventure; surely it would give her a refreshing insight into her own future. The burden of Alisha's deceit would become history and she need not worry over something she was not responsible for.

"Mother! Good news!"

"Curtis, tell me!"

"I've passed the LSAT *and* I will be a first-year law student at Harvard."

"Oh, son, I'm so happy and so proud of you!"

"Thanks, Mom!"

"Where will you be living?"

"I've heard about an apartment in Cambridge, near Central Square, and I've been online . . . think I've lined up a roommate. We've been sending e-mails back and forth, he's from California, but I think he got his undergraduate degree from Tufts University. We've traded photos, and although he says he's Nisei, born in America, you know, his folks, I think, not sure, were born in Japan.

But, Mom, it's the funniest thing," Curtis went on to tell his mother, "except for his hair and slightly slanted eyes, he looks like us."

"You're kidding! But in this day and age, Curtis, anything is possible."

"Tell me about it," Curtis said, thinking about his parents' divorce. "Well, Mom, gotta go . . . just wanted to give you *my* good news. Is Jane okay?"

"Oh, my, yes, she'll be pleased with your good news. I know she will. Keep in touch and bring your new friend over for dinner anytime, love to have you."

Curtis had planned to meet Bob Sato at the well-known bar and grill in Harvard Square. Because they had exchanged e-mails and photographs, he almost felt as if he was meeting an old friend. The summer-long communications had made it possible for him to feel that way and he was looking forward to meeting Bob Sato.

The room was crowded, filled with chatting students milling about, greeting one another. He approached the maitre d' while scanning the room.

"May I help you, sir?"

"Yes, I'm meeting a friend. Oh, I think I see him."

"Fine." Picking up two menus, the host followed Curtis to the table.

Bob Sato stood, having recognized Curtis when he reached the table, and extended his hand.

"How are you doing?" Curtis asked. "When did you get in?"

"Been here in Cambridge for two days."

"You should have called me; could have gotten together sooner."

"Well, you see, after graduation, I went back to California to spend some time with my folks."

"I can understand that. It's good to meet you at last, Bob."

"So, what do you want to eat?" Curtis asked.

"American food, and plenty of it."

"I'm with you on that."

Both men studied their menus and when their waiter approached, Curtis said, "I'm having steak."

Bob said, "I'd like steak as well."

The waiter took their orders, each having steak, medium well-done, with Curtis opting for French fries and Bob ordering rice. And both ordered a fresh garden salad and a beer.

"So, where are you staying, Bob?"

"For now, I'm at The Charles Hotel."

"Everything all right there?"

"Sure. It's comfortable, but I'm hoping that soon we can move into the apartment you found in Cambridge."

"It's not far from where we are right now. After we eat we can go, take a look at it. Are you ready to sign a lease for a year?"

"I'm ready, but the rent has to be reasonable. My dad will help me out, but I'd rather not have to ask him, you know . . ."

"I understand. I'll be trying to find a part-time job to help with expenses myself," Curtis said, frowning as he thought about his parents.

With the divorce there would be very little money for him. The trust fund his father had provided for him would not be available to him until he became twenty-five, two years away.

But working would not be new to him. All through high school and college he had worked as a camp counselor, mowed lawns, shoveled snow, worked in small factories, even worked as an orderly (courtesy of his dad) in hospitals, finally getting a job he liked as a reporter for the town weekly.

He had saved some money, and his mother promised to help. The Cape property had been deeded to Curtis and his sister; his mom suggested they rent it out for the year and that money would help. Leanne told her son, "I have contacts that will manage the place for a small fee. Because there's no mortgage, that should help both you and your sister."

Curtis readily agreed, knowing his sister wanted to work toward a master's degree in education.

He told Bob, "All my life I've worked, even though my dad is a doctor. I always tried to be independent, take pride in taking care of myself."

"My dad ran a farm in San Diego, and I always worked on the farm."

"What kind of farm?"

"Mainly fruits and vegetables. You know, tomatoes, corn, potatoes, melons, peppers, all types of squash."

"Must have been hard work."

"Back-breaking, that's what it was, Curtis. I vowed I would do something else with *my* life."

Curtis had been cutting a piece of steak and looked up at his new friend and shook his head with understanding. "Can see why you would want to do that."

"I'm the oldest of three, two brothers, so I had to help," Bob told him.

"Did you pay your own way through college?" Curtis asked him.

"With scholarships and part-time work in a computer store."

"In a way I guess all that has prepared you for really hard work," Curtis said. "I'm expecting this first year is going to be hard."

"So I've heard," Bob said as he crossed his fork and knife over his cleaned plate, then reached for his wallet, from which he took several large bills.

Noticing this, Curtis picked up the bill the waiter had left.

"Split this down the middle?"

"Fine. I'm anxious to see the apartment."

As they walked to Curtis's car, which was parked on a side street, Curtis couldn't get over his new friend's physique. Curtis himself was six feet, two inches, but Bob was nearly as tall. Six feet at least, Curtis figured, and he had a robust, bulky build, strong bones. Curtis realized he was making stereotypical judgments based on what he thought Japanese people should look like. He spoke up.

"Bob, how tall are you?"

His new friend laughed.

"Thought all Japanese were short, eh? Believe it or not, Curtis, my man, you and I are closer than you think. My mother is a proud African-American woman. All four of her brothers are over six feet, five inches, and played college basketball. My folks met at a basketball game . . . and, well, here I am."

Curtis laughed. "Guilty as charged, making the wrong assumptions. Please accept my apology. Stereotyping is not a good thing."

"No problem," Bob said as they reached Curtis's car, a Jeep Cherokee.

"Like your car," Bob told him as they got in and fastened their seatbelts.

"It's been good. Not new, but for a five-year-old, I'm not complaining."

The drive to Western Avenue was a short one, and in no time they were front of a Victorian type residence.

"We're here, our new home away from home."

"Nice house," Bob observed.

"I think so," Curtis said. "The woman who owns it, a Mrs. Alexis Lockett, mostly uses it as a bed and breakfast, but she has an apartment on the third floor that she likes to reserve for tenants like us, short-time residents."

"I like the looks of it, Curtis. A nice wrap-around porch . . . would you say it was Victorian style?"

"Guess so, although I don't know too much about house designs. But it's a nice tan color and the fieldstone foundation tells me it's substantial. Let's go have a look. Mrs. Lockett is expecting us."

They walked up the front steps to the porch, which had several wooden rockers and a few tables, suggesting it was a comfortable place to relax.

CHAPTER 23

Curtis rang the bell beside a heavy glass-paned oak door and saw a figure approaching down a well-lit hall.

"You must be my new law school students," she greeted them. "Come in, come in and make yourselves at home."

"I'm Curtis Matthews and this is Bob Sato, Mrs. Lockett."

Curtis thought Mrs. Lockett might be about sixty years old. She was a round-faced woman of medium height and weight. Her bright smile, sparkling brown eyes and tawny skin tones made him think of a typical grandmother.

She led them into the living room.

"Let's sit down and get acquainted," she said, "and I can tell you about my home."

Both men made appropriate remarks as they settled themselves on a comfortable sofa. Mrs. Lockett stood facing them.

"May I offer you a cold drink, ice tea, lemonade, ginger ale?"

"Thanks, but we've just had lunch," Curtis told her, but looked over at Bob, who shook his head. "No thanks, ma'am."

"It would be no problem," she persisted.

"Well, in that case, lemonade sounds good. Bob?"

"Right. Thanks, ma'am."

"Be right back."

Within minutes she returned with a wooden tray with three tall glasses of lemonade, napkins and a plate of assorted cookies.

As she entered the room, Bob went over to her.

"Let me take that, Mrs. Lockett."

"Fine, Bob, is it?"

"Yes, ma'am."

"Please put it on the coffee table and you both help yourselves," she said and smiled.

But Bob brought a glass and a napkin to her before sitting down on the sofa with his own glass and napkin. He had selected a few cookies as well.

"I expect you young men would like to see the apartment. But let me tell you about my home. My husband and I bought this house about thirty years ago and opened it as a bed and breakfast. As you can well imagine, Cambridge is a college town and we have had many guests, parents bringing their children to college, and then returning for their graduation. Each room has its own bathroom, and breakfast is always served 'do it yourself' style from six a.m. to nine-thirty a.m. You know, plenty of hot coffee, cereal, doughnuts, muffins, toast, fresh fruit in season, that sort of fare. But on Sundays I serve a brunch-style breakfast from nine to eleven for people who signed up on Saturday evening."

"Sounds good to me," Curtis said, "especially the brunch."

"But I expect, from what you said on the phone, you want to see the apartment."

They nodded and she continued.

"I've set up the third floor, a large attic, as a two bed-room and bath apartment with a small kitchen. Also, there is a back flight of stairs with a key-entry steel door. It faces an alley, and that's why we installed the protective door. Of course you may use the front entrance if you wish. I will give you keys for that door."

She went to a desk in the corner of the living room and returned with a manila folder. "I'll give each of you a copy of this set of rules when you sign your lease. I do have a few: no smoking, no drinking, no parties or overnight guests . . . of either sex. And there will be a lease signed by each of you with the rent being $1,300 each, with $500 security deposit from each of you. The rent is payable on the first of each month."

"Sounds good to me," Curtis said.

"Would you like to see it?" she asked.

"Yes, we would." Bob gathered the empty glasses and placed them on the tray.

"Shall I take these to the kitchen?"

"Oh, no, son. Leave the tray. I'll get it later. Want you to see where you'll be living while you wrestle with those big old law books."

"You know, Curtis, I'm glad that we have this apart-ment, because I need to have a stable place to live because

I do have regular appointments I have to keep, and I need a place where I can relax and chill out."

"What do you mean, 'regular appointments'? Are you sick? Need treatments?"

Bob shook his head. "No, nothing like that, thank God, but—" He got up, put both of their empty plates into the kitchen sink, returned to his seat.

Curtis noticed the sober look on Bob's usually smiling, cheerful face. He thought, *This must be something serious.*

"Remember when we were talking about earning money?"

"Yeah, I remember. So?"

"Well, most of the money I earned while was a student at Tufts was as a donor . . ."

"You mean a blood donor?"

Bob did not answer right away, as if to steel himself for Curtis's reaction. "No, not blood, but I help women have babies . . ."

"God, man! What are you talkin' 'bout? Help women? Are you shittin' me?"

"I donate sperm to sperm banks."

"I'll be damned! And you get paid for . . . for doin' that?"

"I'm very well paid for a few minutes of my time. You know, Curtis, there are a lot of women who want to have children but for some reason or another have not been able to find a male partner. So along with many other men, twice a week for six months I provide semen. I'm paid anywhere from $1,000 to $1,500 a week."

"Man! How did you ever get into this?"

"One of my classmates . . ."

"Man, oh, man, that's something else!"

"Of course I have to pay taxes. And Curtis, my friend, when I get my law degree, my earnings will be much higher."

"And women are willing to pay . . ."

"You'd be surprised. The American Fertility Association says that more and more women are using this service. The numbers say it is a growing field, overall."

"So how long have you been—donating?"

"Past two years."

CHAPTER 24

Obstetrician Joe Collins met them in the admissions area of the hospital and rushed Alisha up to the maternity floor while Don completed the admissions procedure.

By the time Don reached the labor unit, Alisha was in bed being examined by her doctor. He went to the bedside and kissed her damp forehead.

"How are you doing, hon?"

"I'm scared, I'm scared," she wailed.

Dr. Collins finished his examination and, stripping off the glove, he pulled the sheet down over her knees.

Tossing the glove into a waste basket, he said, "Good news! Your wife is a wonder woman—almost seven centimeters dilated!"

He looked up at the large clock on the wall. "I'd say if she keeps progressing, we'll have your son here in a few hours."

Don turned to Alisha, exclaiming, "Hear that, hon! Won't be long now."

He, too, looked up at the clock on the wall. It was almost three. Alisha had started her labor at one. With luck, he though, the child would be born by dawn. *The dawn of a new day, a new life.*

A half hour later the doctor returned to check his patient's progress, with Don watching him closely, grinning as he saw the doctor's satisfied nod.

A nurse came to Don.

"Should get you ready for the delivery. I'll take you to the scrub room so you can suit up."

"I understand," he said, turning to his wife. "Alisha, I'm going to get into scrubs, but I'll be right back. Don't go anywhere," he teased. She responded with a muffled moan.

By the time Don was in the operating room garb, Alisha had been moved to the delivery room and was receiving a spinal anesthesia.

When that was done, Don was told by a nurse to sit on a stool near Alisha's head. She asked, "Do you need anything?"

"No, thanks, not at the moment."

His whispered to Alisha, "You are doing very well, my dear."

"I can't *do* this, Don, I can't," she moaned.

"Of course you can. Just breathe normally and work with us when we count down. You *can* do it, I know you can."

A few minutes later she appeared to be focusing on the task at hand. Her face was quite red, her mouth in a tight grimace, and she began to respond to Don and the nurses' encouragement. As the count progressed from one to ten, she exerted herself, held her breath and pushed.

From his position at the foot of the delivery table, Dr. Collins coached her. "The head is crowning. After a few more good pushes, your baby will be here. Take a deep breath and give me one good push!"

The head presented, then the shoulders, and seconds later the baby's body emerged. The baby's strong cry filled the room as Dr. Collins handed Don a pair of sterile scissors to cut the cord. As his son was being wrapped in a receiving blanket, he leaned over, kissing Alisha.

"He's beautiful! You did a great job!"

The baby was cleaned, weighed, treated according to standard newborn procedures. He was handed to Don, who took the baby to show him to his mother.

"Here's John Morton Matthews to say 'hello' to Mommy," he said. She closed her eyes, turning her face away.

Stunned by her reaction, he pressed on.

"This is your baby, Alisha!"

Her head still turned, she mumbled, "Take him away, I don't want him!"

Don persisted, unable to understand this strange and decidedly unexpected reaction. "Look at your baby!"

Her voice was icy, but quite calm.

"Not my baby. Yours!"

Dr. Collins watched his distressed colleague return the baby to the nurse, who immediately transferred the infant to the nursery.

He beckoned Don to follow him out of the delivery room.

"I know Alisha's behavior is very upsetting to you, but for her this seemed to have been a very traumatic experience. Doesn't happen often, but we do see it occasionally. I'm going to prescribe a sedative for her right away and we'll see how she does. We'll keep a close eye on her. It's not uncommon for new mothers to disassociate from the experience."

"It's so important that the mother bonds with her baby right away. It's vital for each of them."

"I know that, Don, I know that. Let me go check on Alisha, she's been transferred to her room. You go see your son in the nursery, then go home. I'll be in touch in the morning. Keep you posted."

The men shook hands, then parted, Don to the nursery and Dr. Collins to check on the new mother.

Don stood at the viewing window and watched the nurse walk over to the window with his newborn son in her arms. He was a healthy seven-pound baby with toast brown skin and glossy black hair. The nurse had taken the knit cap off so that Don could see it. His eyes were tightly closed, but Don noticed a decided slant to them, a slightly oriental look.

He gestured to the nurse to show him the baby's fingers and toes, which were decidedly short and stubby. The Matthews family had always been teased about their long fingers and toes.

Must be from Alisha's side of the family. As he recalled, Mr. Morton's hands were good-sized with short, stubby fingers. And he was a steel mill worker. Maybe that accounted for the size. *But, no, that wouldn't make his fingers short.* Don then left the hospital and got into his car to drive home. What was wrong with him? Alisha! Her toes and fingers were short and stubby!

What's the matter with me? Am I trying to deny my own child?

By the time he pulled into the driveway, the sun was rising in the east with glorious red tints in the pearl-gray sky.

As he put his key into the front door lock, he prayed silently. *Please, God, let all be well. Please.*

CHAPTER 25

Once inside his house, Don went upstairs. He needed a quick shower, then to bed. Before he went into the bathroom, he called the hospital to check on his wife. He had asked for and secured a private nurse to be with Alisha for a day or two. When the nurse, a Mrs. Sparks, answered, she told him, "Mrs. Matthews is doing well, vital signs normal, and she is sleeping right now." After thanking her for her help, he went right to the shower and then to bed, falling asleep the moment his head hit the pillow.

When he awoke, it was noon, and at first he felt somewhat disoriented, but the previous day's activities flooded into his mind. He reached for the bedside telephone, anxious to find out how Alisha was doing.

"Oh, yes, Dr. Matthews, we're doing nicely," Mrs. Sparks said."Yes," she said when he asked about the baby, "he's right here with his mother. She's breastfeeding him right now."

"That's great! Tell Mrs. Matthews I'll be there within the hour, and ask her if she needs anything."

"She says 'no,' Dr. Matthews. Just bring yourself," she said and laughed.

Don dressed in gray slacks, a white tee shirt and a navy blazer, drank a glass of milk, ate some crackers and left for the hospital.

He stopped at the florist shop for a bouquet of pink and white roses for his wife. As he drove, feelings of relief swirled all through him knowing that Alisha had finally accepted her child. What would he have done if she had totally rejected the child?

The very thought made him shudder. He decided to ask Mrs. Sparks if she could help out for a few days at their home.

He really had to get back to his practice, which seemed to be on the upturn with new patients.

When he got to Alisha's room, he was delighted to find her sitting on a rocker with her baby in her arms.

"Shh-h," she smiled when he came over, kissed her and pecked at the sleeping infant.

"Isn't he beautiful?" she whispered.

"Sure is. Most beautiful one I've seen in a long time." He handed her the flowers. "These are for you."

"Thanks, Don, they're lovely."

"I'll see to these," Mrs. Sparks said. "See if I can find a vase."

"How *are* you feeling, Alisha?"

"Fine. A little tired, but I don't remember giving birth or anything!"

Don was completely surprised at what she'd said, remembering her strange behavior the night before.

"Don't you remember *anything*?"

"Only the ride to the hospital and Dr. Collins pushing me in the wheelchair to the maternity unit. All the rest is a blur."

"Well," he hastened to reassure her, "you did fine! Great! Honey, you hit it right out of the ballpark. A home run all the way!"

"I did? You're just saying that!"

"No, no, you were outstanding. You went from seven centimeters dilation to full dilation in an hour, and then no freight train could have stopped you! You were awesome!"

Mrs. Sparks tapped on the door, came in with the roses in a crystal vase, and in her other arm a beautiful arrangement of fall flowers.

"These are from your staff, Dr. Matthews."

"They are very nice." He thought that very likely Becky had initiated the gesture.

Mrs. Sparks took the baby from Alisha and returned him to his bassinet, which had been brought to Alisha's room. The infant would be returned to the nursery after the evening feeding so that his mother could get a good night's sleep.

When he returned home, Don put in a call to Joe Collins.

"Joe? Don here. Man, you're some kind of a miracle worker! I've just left Alisha and she's doing fine. What a turnaround! She's breastfeeding. What miracle drug did you order?"

"As I told you, Don, the condition your wife was in . . . somehow the labor and delivery . . . having a baby, expelling seven pounds of a human being from her body, was an extremely traumatic experience for her. And I knew that if we could get her over that hurdle, past that . . ."

"So, you sedated her?"

"Yes, indeed. Years ago we would use an opiate, along with another drug that would temporarily block out any memory of the painful experience."

"Now that you mention it, I do remember in med school, during my OB-GYN rotation, hearing something like that. Not used much anymore. We have more sophisticated drugs these days."

"Right, but there are times when an older generation of drugs may fit the need perfectly."

"Don't know how to thank you, Joe."

"Just be happy, Don, that's all. Be happy."

"Thanks, Joe, for everything."

"No problem," Joe said as he hung up.

Alisha's plans were to take Baby Jay, as they called him, "J" for John, her father's name, to visit her parents in Pittsburgh. Don could not go because he was trying to catch up on missed patients' appointments.

The baby had a very happy, placid disposition and was beginning to recognize and respond to his parents with smiles and bubbly sounds.

Alisha, too, had noted the peculiar slant of her son's eyes, as well as the dark wisps of black, straight hair that added to his faintly Asian appearance. Silently she worried, *Had the sperm bank made the wrong selection? How much would Jay's appearance change as he grew older? Would Don notice?*

So far Don had been pleased with the baby's growth and development. He seemed to be reliving the joys and happy moments he'd had with his two other children. She knew that her husband had felt deep disappointment at their response when he informed Curtis and Jane of the birth of their half brother. He'd sent out announcements to friends and co-workers. His children's reply was a curt "congratulations." He was upset, but could understand their feelings.

And then there were times when little Jay would seem to be looking at Don with questions in his dark brown, almost black, slightly slanted eyes. His hair seemed untamable, standing up in coarse, wiry spikes despite his mother's attempts to control it with baby oil.

"His hair is much like yours, Alisha," he told her. "Sometimes he almost looks oriental, with that hair and eyes."

"I never told you, I guess," Alisha lied, "there is oriental blood in my family."

"I didn't know that!"

She looked at her husband to access his reaction to this unexpected news.

He seemed thoughtful, then responded, "That could account for the slight Asian look that Jay has. But I've never, in *my* practice, figured that a genetic predisposition would be so evident . . ."

"You see, Don, my mother's father, my grandfather, was from Jamaica. And as I understand it, there were many Japanese and Chinese immigrants who intermarried with the native women, and I think my grandfather's name was Tom Shikako when he brought the family to Alabama, where Momma was born."

"Who knows," Don conceded, "there might be Asians in *my* family."

"You never know, I guess. Do you have a family tree?"

"I only knew my grandparents on my father's side of the family. I always said I was going to do some DNA research to see what I could find out. Today many are using DNA to find out where they really come from."

Alisha shivered as if a creepy chill had crept over her body. She had had to think quickly to come up with a name for a mythical Japanese ancestor.

CHAPTER 26

John Morton was delighted with his new grandson and especially pleased with the way his wife reacted to the child. Seemingly, she couldn't get enough of him. Eager to hold him, feed him, change him. It was as if a fairy wand had touched her and returned her to her old self.

Alisha told her father, "It is as if she is back to when I was a baby . . ."

"I know, and I'm worried about how she will behave when you leave and take him away."

"I'm afraid she'll think I'm stealing *her* baby," Alisha said. "We may have to sneak him out. But then, Dad, how will you handle Mom? She's sure to be upset and act out. If I'd known this was going to happen, I wouldn't have come home with him."

He hugged her. "But I'm very glad you did. I'll manage your mother, somehow. So what does your husband think of his son?" John Morton asked.

"He's very pleased, Dad, although he's not able to spend too much time with us, busy with his practice and all that . . ." Her voice trailed off. Her father took notice of this and picking up on her somber tone, asked, "And you, honey, are you happy?"

"Yes, Dad, I am," she replied quickly. "I have what I've always wanted—a wonderful husband, a child, and a home of my own. Who wouldn't be happy?"

"Well, honey, you know I only want the best for you, and I'm glad you're happy with your life."

Still he wondered. Young John Morton Matthews did not resemble anyone in *his* family, or in his wife Maribel's family. How had his grandson come by the slightly slanted eyes, the dark black, coarse, wiry hair?

Although her father had admired the baby, cuddled him, talked to him, there was a certain lack of exuberance, Alisha had noticed, as if her father was trying too hard. Alisha thought he was not as effusive as his wife. Alisha saw the questions in her father's eyes. She began to worry. Now both her husband and her father had made references to her son's physical appearance. *Had the donor clinic made an error in selecting the sperm donation?* she wondered, and worried more.

She knew she had been explicit in what she wanted, an African-American, well educated, a professional, excellent mental and physical health, between the ages of twenty-five and thirty-five.

She could only hope that Don had accepted the lie she had told him about the distant Japanese relative.

Don seemed happy with his young son, and quite proud, as well. He was constantly taking pictures, showing them to friends and colleagues. So far he seemed proud of his second son, although he still wondered about the possibility of a genetic strain passing down through four generations. His delight in being able to produce had boosted his ego tremendously. Even so, he did miss his relationship with his two older children.

One evening after Jay had been put to bed—he was now sleeping through the night—Don mentioned his disappointment to his wife.

"I'm upset that my children seem to have little interest in their new brother."

Alisha had been knitting a blanket for the baby. She put the work down in her lap, recognized the glum look on her husband's face, said to him, "I think I can understand, because I think it's probably their ages and this time in their lives when they are mostly concerned with themselves, going to college, starting new careers . . ."

"But, Alisha, he's *their* brother, a part of their family."

"They don't see it that way, I guess. *Their* family was you and Leanne. You should keep sending pictures of Jay to them, and as he changes and grows, I'm sure their attitude will change."

Don didn't notice how quickly his wife lowered her head, picked up her work and resumed knitting. *What will I do if Don ever learns what I've done?*

Thinking back to the time of his son's conception, Don was certain he had used a condom, but he didn't really remember. Had it been defective? Jay *had* to be his child, and he did look like his mother, the same tawny skin tone, the same black, steel-wiry hair. Only the baby's hair seemed coarser, not as soft as Alisha's. But the eyes! Don couldn't help wondering, *four* generations? Don knew what he had to do. Some medical research was in order to satisfy his doubt.

He decided to say nothing to Alisha, but he had to know. He would search for a geneticist, and check online for starters.

Don did not know it, but there was someone else who had noticed the unusual features of her boss' son.

Becky had seen the photograph of the three-month-old Jay Matthews alongside the high school photos of his older half siblings. The difference was noticeable to her, but she kept her thoughts to herself. Up to now, Dr. Matthews had appeared pleased with his son's progress and spoke often about the baby's growth and development in glowing terms.

"He recognizes me and his mother, breaks out in smiles whenever we talk to him. He's a bright, healthy baby and we are real proud of him," he said one day at the end of the staff meeting. "I'm so lucky to be the father of such a wonderful child."

Still, Becky wondered. Could Alisha have Asian genes in her gene pool, and how about Dr. Matthews? Could he? Becky remembered once hearing about a married couple . . . each of whom had had a rhinoplasty, but neither revealed to the other that his/her nose had been surgically altered. When their first child was born, they had to worry about more than their son's circumcision.

Leanne's living room in her new house was just a few steps from the front door, down a carpeted hall on the left side. It was a comfortable, relaxing room with a white

Berber carpet, a small blue and gold oriental rug beneath a marble coffee table. There was a deep wine-colored sofa, a pair of wing chairs in front of the fireplace. All made for a 'welcome home' feeling.

Leanne led her son and his guest into the room. She pointed to the sofa. "Please, make yourselves comfortable. Just have a few more touches for our dinner."

"And," Curtis asked, "what's for dinner, Mom? Chicken cacciatore?"

"That's right, with rice . . ."

Curtis turned to Bob. "Bob, you're in for some good eating!"

"Sounds great to me. Mrs. Matthews, can I help?" Bob asked.

"Not at all. I'll be right back with a couple of cold beers."

"Sure I can't help?" Bob insisted.

She smiled. "Maybe later, cleaning up, you know."

"No problem. I know my way 'round a kitchen."

Leanne returned in a few minutes with a tray that she placed on the coffee table. Bob Sato made room by moving a few magazines aside. On the tray were the beers and a bowl of pretzels.

"Have at it," she told them, waving aside their thanks.

"So, Bob, Curtis tells me that you are part African-American, as well as Japanese. He also told me that you are the perfect roommate . . . and I want you to know that's a *lot*, coming from my picky son," she laughed.

Curtis, giving his mother an *"Oh, Ma,"* look, said, "Well, Bob is an okay guy, and we hit it off right away."

"You know, Mrs. Matthews, it seems that Curtis and I were destined to meet, and I for one feel that we'll be friends for a long time. Hope so, anyway," he added.

"That would be great," Leanne said. "Before I go to check on a few more things in the kitchen, I would love to hear more about your family. You're originally from California?"

"That's right, ma'am. We've lived in Pasadena most of my life. My mom is African-American and from Texas. Her folks left there to find work. My dad ran a small vegetable farm and my two brothers and I worked with him—that is, until we finished high school. And I tell you, Mrs. Matthews, that not one of us is interested in farming. Think that's why all of us came east for college."

"All three of you?" Leanne asked.

"Yes, ma'am, all three. I started at Tufts in pre-dentistry, changed to pre-law. Caleb, the brother next to me, is a junior in accounting at Babson. And the youngest brother, Morris, is at Syracuse University in New York. He is on a full football scholarship . . . not in basketball, but my father was happy with football."

"I'm sure he must be very proud of all of you."

Curtis wondered what his mother would think if she ever found out how Bob supported himself through college, and even now in law school. For himself, he was having a hard time getting his mind around the idea of Bob being a sperm donor. *God, after all this time, how many children does he have out there in the world?*

147

CHAPTER 27

Concerned that Jay bore no resemblance to either of his other children, Don had decided that DNA testing would be the only way to get a definite answer to the questions plaguing him.

He had gone online to obtain the necessary DNA kit. It contained the materials for the cheek swabbing, instructions and addresses for nearby laboratories that could process the samples and report the findings. The kit also included instructions on how to package the material to be tested. The lab's report would be mailed back to him in a plain brown envelope with no return address to protect the inquirer's privacy.

One night after dinner Alisha said she needed to go to the drugstore.

"I have a few things I need to pick up, some for me and some for the baby," she told Don. "Won't be gone long."

"Take your time, we'll be fine," he assured her.

As soon as he was sure she had gone, he picked the baby up from the playpen and carried him into the master bedroom. Holding the child in one arm, he laid out the contents of the kit. He had already swabbed his own cheek before leaving his office.

He talked to the gurgling, happy baby when he sat down beside him on the bed. "You're a dear, sweet little boy, but I'm not sure you're mine."

Chucking Jay under his chin, he swabbed his inner cheek and placed the sample in the container that had been provided.

He sealed the kit as instructed and placed it in his medical bag.

For the next three weeks, he fretted endlessly, barely able to act normal around Alisha and the baby.

In response to her query, "What's wrong with you, Don? You seem so worried, so jumpy, is everything all right at the clinic?"

"It's my patient load," he told her. "Increasing to the point that it seems that each patient session is taking more and more time. Backup is almost too much to handle. I'm really bushed at the end of the day, especially when I have to check on my hospitalized patients."

"I understand," she said.

He said nothing, but his anxiety increased as he waited for the DNA results. He began to worry, too, if there could be some kind of genetic mutation causing the distinctly Asian features the baby might have inherited.

When Alisha returned from shopping, she told Don about Jay's visit to the pediatrician.

"Dr. Blume says that Jay is right on target."

"Well, that's good to hear."

"Said our son is very healthy, growing nicely, and that we can start him on baby food with the bottle, as needed."

"That's great!"

"I think so, too, because, well, Don, I'd like to go back to finish my degree program."

"Why? Why, Leanne never . . ."

He caught himself mid-sentence, but not before Alisha knew exactly what he was going to say.

He did not miss the sarcasm in her voice. "Of course, the wonderful Leanne *never* left her children!"

"She never had to. Nor do you!"

"I want my own career, thank you very much!"

Noting the look of defiance in her voice and on her face, Don thought of how their lives had changed. What was wrong with the woman? He thought she had what she wanted; marriage to him, a child, a home of her own. He had not acknowledged a certain truth that he'd recognized some time ago. And that was Alisha's diminished interest in any sexual activity. Her overactive sexual appetite had not returned. After her postpartum recovery, she seemed much less interested in any sexual activity, proclaiming that it was too soon. The physician in Don thought, *this is strange behavior.* Although he was not an obstetrician, he knew that most healthy women were eager to resume normal sexual activity. And, certainly, early on his wife had shown him a vigorous sexual appetite.

This rejecting of intimacy, combined with her latest announcement of "returning to educational pursuits," made him wonder what next new change would she bring into their lives.

He did not voice his misgivings but instead began to question her about her going back to school. He sighed deeply. "How do you propose to manage care for Jay?" he asked.

She laughed. "You mean you've forgotten that your own medical facility has a child care center right on the first floor?"

"Guess so. Never had to use it, so it never concerned me."

"Several female doctors on staff use the facility, as well as do some nurses. And I do know that the child care center does take infants, as well as toddlers."

Don pushed back from the table and went into the living room. She followed him. "I'd rather you stay at home with him. At least until he's walking."

"I should think you'd be pleased, Don," she countered. "He'll be right down on the first floor . . . you could check on him anytime you want."

"Could be," he grudgingly agreed. "It *would* be good for one of us to be close by."

"Right, that's what I thought, too."

"What's this day care going to cost?"

"It's $800 a month. A five-day week with expanded hours from seven in the morning until six in the evening. We have to sign a contract stipulating a week's notice should we want to terminate the contract."

"I see. So when do we sign this contract?" he asked her, suddenly weary of the discussion. "And when do we start Jay's day care?" He was not at all happy with his wife's arbitrary decision, but decided he would wait until he knew the DNA test results before he made any decisions.

Using the Internet, he had located an agency that would provide a Y chromosome analysis to prove whether or not the male Y chromosome had been handed down from father to son.

Nearly a month of agonizing tension passed before the brown envelope with no return address arrived in his office mail. It was hidden in a pile of junk mail.

He tried to control himself, but nervous perspiration flooded down his face, almost blinding his eyesight. His hands were trembling and clammy as he extracted the envelope, came upon the information that could change his life once again.

He stuffed the unsorted pile of mail into his desk drawer. He then locked the door to his office and took the envelope into his bathroom. He closed the toilet seat lid and placed the envelope on it. Turning on the cold water, he splashed water over his face several times until he felt relieved. After patting his face and hands dry, he picked up the envelope. Sitting down on the closed toilet seat, he opened it.

Scanning quickly through the one-page letter, his eyes widened, his attention riveted to the summary at the bottom of the page.

DNA test results of tissue samples Number 41818 and 41819 show there is no match in their Y chromosomes, therefore no paternal link.

The report was signed by a Robert Goodman, M.D. Don leaned back against the cool toilet tank. *Goodman, how appropriate. You really are my good man!*

He took a deep breath. Glancing at his watch, he knew he had four or five scheduled patients to see. But he decided that with this development in his life, he needed legal advice.

He went into his office and secured his letter in his briefcase, unlocked his office door and put in a call to Frank Jones, his lawyer and long-time friend.

CHAPTER 28

"Frank, I'm so glad you could make the time to see me."

"Don, it's always good to see you, anytime. What can I do for you?"

Don took a seat that Frank Jones offered him and lowered his face into his hands, shaking his head. In a voice tight with emotion, he mumbled, "Frank, I don't know how I could have been such a damn fool."

His bleary eyes, dejection and desperation on his face told the lawyer that his client and friend was in some serious difficulty.

"Tell me about your problem," the lawyer encouraged Don.

"Look, Frank, here I am, a board-certified primary care physician with a thriving practice, a wonderful wife of twenty-five years, two precious, smart children, and I turned my back on all of that . . . for sex! What happened to me? And now what's *going* to happen to me?"

He stared out of the window behind the lawyer's desk as if trying to gain some sort of perspective from the vibrant fall scene of maple trees with glorious crowns of gold and red leaves, the dark green of pine trees, the cotton white clouds moving slowly across the cerulean sky. But the peaceful scene seemed to be mocking him.

His lawyer pulled a legal pad from his desk drawer and quietly said, "Don, calm down. Tell me what your problem is all about." He poured his friend a glass of water from his desk carafe and waited expectantly.

"Thanks, man," Don said, taking the entire glass of water in several gulps. "I needed that."

"Welcome. Can you continue now? I realize that this is hard, but take it slow. I do know that you remarried shortly after your divorce from Leanne . . . ."

"Biggest mistake I've ever made."

"Let's take it from there."

With a deep sigh Don said, "Right. Alisha and I got married in Pittsburgh at her parents' home. She, well, we had been sexually active for a few months, and although I always used protection . . . but you know as well as I do that imperfections can happen, but still I was in denial when she told me she was pregnant."

"Did you think that was a possibility?"

"No. At first I thought it could not be possible, not at all."

"So it was when you realized that she *was* really pregnant . . ."

"I had to ask Leanne for a divorce and tell her why."

It seemed to Frank that reliving that moment was going to completely unravel whatever composure Don had managed to hold onto. He wanted to direct Don closer to the problem at hand.

Frank interrupted, hoping that would steer Don closer to revealing his problem. "So you got the divorce, married Alisha, and she had the baby."

"Frank, that should have been a clue to me! When I think of it now . . . how stupid I was."

Frank looked up from his pad. "What should have been a clue?"

"Her instability. Right after the child's birth, immediately, when I took him to her, she refused to look at the baby. Said to me 'Not *my* baby, yours!' And she turned her face away. I was stunned."

"So what happened? She finally accepted the baby?"

"The doctor seemed to recognize the problem, prescribed a sedative, a drug known as a hypnotic, erased any memory of the delivery the night before. The next day when I went to see her and the baby, she was *fine*. Was actually trying to breastfeed him."

"That was good, wasn't it?"

"Well, yes, for the baby, but when I really looked at the baby, it seemed to me that he should have had some resemblance to my other children."

"He didn't look like either of them?"

"I didn't expect he would look exactly like Curtis or Jane, after all . . . different mothers, but this child had what I thought was a decided Asian slant to his eyes, and his hair was jet black, abundant, and had a coarse texture. But when I mentioned this to Alisha, she said something about having a Japanese grandfather. Frank . . ."

"What, Don?"

"That child is *not* mine!"

"How do you know?"

"Read this." Don took out the brown envelope from his briefcase.

Looking sober, the lawyer read the findings, then passed the document back to Don.

"Have you told Alisha?"

"I've wanted to confront her, but I thought I should have legal advice, so here I am. What a mess I've made of my life."

"Don't worry, Don, we'll sort it out. I presume you do not wish to remain in this marriage now."

"Are you kidding me? Damn straight!" Don sputtered, his eyes widening.

"To begin with, I need to make a copy of that report. And I suggest you put the original in a secure place, like your safety deposit box at your bank. What I can tell you now is that you are the baby's *legal* father, although not his *biological* father. I'm going to be checking case law to determine what we do next. But you should inform your wife of your discovery, and also let her know you have retained legal counsel to pursue a divorce. But be mindful, you still may be responsible for the child's support."

Don stared at Frank. "Even though he is *not* my biological child?"

"You were legally married to his mother at the time of his birth, and your name is listed as his father on his birth certificate."

Rattled by the idea that he might be responsible for support of a child that was not his, Don willed himself to listen carefully to his lawyer.

"Thank you, Frank. I'll certainly do as you suggest and put the original in my safety deposit box. It is secure. Alisha does not have a key."

"That's good, Don, but it might be wise to have a second secure box, just in case. God forbid something should happen to you. You need to protect yourself."

"I know. So far, Frank, I've done nothing but make horrible mistakes in my life."

"Okay," lawyer advised, "let's make sure no new ones are made. I want you to be very careful about how you approach your wife with this information. I know you are upset and angry, but as a professional man you must keep your cool. We will get you back on track, trust me. Just don't do anything foolish. You know what I mean."

Driving home from his lawyer's office, Don knew that he faced a big problem. Obviously, Alisha had had an affair with someone and blamed her pregnancy on him. He realized that he had to start to think the way he had been taught in medical school. First, assess the problem. Second, put all the facts, as he knew them, together. Third, make a plan of action that would resolve the situation. He began thinking about what he would say to Alisha and how he would handle her reaction when he confronted her.

Don was so distraught, so flushed and perspiring so much that he had to turn on the car's air conditioning. He slowed down as he neared the turn into his street. Although he was not what could be called a praying man, he searched his mind for some type of invocation to soothe his troubled mind. All he could think of was the Lord's Prayer, so he recited it, hoping it would help.

He drove into the driveway and was surprised by how serene and normal everything looked. He'd almost expected some form of disarray to be evident. As soon as he entered the house, he called, "Alisha, where are you?"

"In the kitchen, feeding Jay."

"I've got to talk to you right now!"

"What about? What's the matter?"

When she looked at his face, she knew that she was in trouble, but she tried to act normally, as if to delay the inevitable. She wiped the baby's mouth and placed him in his playpen and gave him a toy before looking at Don. "What's your problem?"

"My problem?" he shouted. He thought he was going to explode, he was so angry, but he remembered Frank's words of caution. He made himself take a deep breath. If he could just remain calm, he would be able to move forward with the situation facing him.

"Sit down. I have some questions for you."

Alisha did as told, and Don saw anxiety and tension creeping over her face. He went right to the point.

"Who did you sleep with before I married you?"

"No one, no one, never slept with anyone but you!"

"Liar! Liar!" Don pulled the brown envelope from his briefcase. "No one? Well, read *this*!" he demanded, thrusting the brown envelope at her. "Read this and explain it to me."

As she read the DNA report her eyes grew large and she could barely speak. In a shaking voice that was barely above a whisper, she said, "I—I used a donor."

"You used a *what*? A sperm donor? Just to have a baby and lie that it was my child?" Almost involuntarily he clenched his fists and started to move toward her, but the fear in her eyes made him recall Frank's warning. "Be careful, don't do anything foolish."

Her face hidden in her hands, she mumbled, "I love you, Don. Always have loved you, and I was, was desperate!"

"Why, you lying bitch! I gave up my wonderful wife and family and almost destroyed my practice to do right by you and the child. And you go and have a baby by someone you don't even know! No wonder Jay looks different!"

"I'm sorry, I'm sorry. I asked the clinic for someone that fit you, looked like you . . ."

"Well, you didn't find him!"

As he glared at a weeping Alisha, Don knew that if he didn't get away, he might lose control and even attack her—he was that angry.

"What are you going to do?" she asked, lifting her tear-streaked face to him.

"I'm outta here before I do something I will regret. You'll hear from Frank Jones; I've already talked to him!"

He picked up his briefcase, shoved the DNA report into it and turned to leave the kitchen. He planned to pack a few things, not knowing where he was going, but as he was leaving the kitchen, the wall telephone rang. He picked it up, thinking it might be a patient.

"This is Dr. Matthews."

"Don?"

The man's voice sounded familiar, and when he said, "Don, is that you?" Don recognized the voice of Alisha's father.

"Mr. Morton? Yes, this is me, Don."

Hearing her father's name Alisha sprang from her chair at the kitchen table and snatched the phone from Don.

"Dad! What's wrong?"

Don watched her as her tear-stained face paled with horror at whatever it was her father was telling her. Don quickly pushed a chair behind her, pressed her shoulders so she could sit down into it. He thought she might faint. He reached for a glass from a cabinet and gave her a glass of water. She was almost struggling to breathe.

"My, God, Dad, when did this happen? Two days? The police?"

Evidently something serious had happened to Alisha's mother. Then he heard Alisha say, "I'll take the first flight I can get. Yes, Dad, I'm coming right away!"

"It's my mother . . . wandered away. I've got to go, my father . . . two days missing! My father needs me!"

"Of course you must go. But what about Jay?"

She looked at Don as if he had lost his mind.

"What about him?"

"Whose going to take care of him?"

"You're not expecting me to take him with me to Pittsburgh? Put him in the day care center, and you can surely manage nights! Listen, do what you want, I'm leaving!"

Though still inwardly seething at Alisha's deception, Don did manage to tell her that he was sorry about her mother and hoped she would be found okay.

"Thanks," she said."I'm going to pack. Call me a taxi, will you?"

"How about money?"

"I have some, and I'll use my credit cards."

Ten minutes later she came downstairs carrying a small overnight bag. She was wearing jeans, a white pullover sweater and a tan quilted car coat, plus a leather bag over her arm.

She ran to the front door to let the driver know she was coming.

Don reminded her about the crisis in their lives, and helping her with her coat, he said to her, "We have serious business to talk about when you get back here."

"I know. I'll call you as soon as I can."

"Good luck."

"Thanks," she said as she got into the taxi.

As if suddenly aware that neither of his parents was nearby, Jay let out a high-pitched wail that announced his distress.

Don rushed into the kitchen and picked the child up. After the wailing stopped, Jay gave Don a toothless smile with a few hiccups.

"Poor little boy. I don't know who your real daddy is, but I do know that he is missing the chance of a lifetime not knowing and loving you. It's not your fault, *none of it*, and I am so sorry that you came into this crazy situation."

He went upstairs to the bedroom, cradling Jay in his arms. Looking at his watch he saw that he had been home less than an hour. Time enough to turn his life upside down. Would he be able to stop it from further spinning out of control?

CHAPTER 29

After months of a nearly unvarying routine of going to work and back to an empty house, Leanne had decided to join a group of divorced women who called themselves First Wives. She learned about the group upon returning some books to the library. As she was leaving, she saw a flyer on the bulletin board in the lobby. *First wives, join us every first Tuesday of the month at eight p.m. in the downstairs community room. Remember, you are not alone. Together we can learn how to cope with divorce.*

Her friend Sharla had been after Leanne for some time, urging her, "Girl, get on with your life! You've got to get out more, meet new people!"

Leanne's response was always, "I know, but it's so hard, Sharla. Easier said than done. What do I do, go up to a stranger, say, 'I'm Leanne Matthews and I'm divorced?' "

Curtis, too, was trying to encourage his mother to get out more.

Leanne thought that neither of them understood her feeling of . . . just floating through life like so much flotsam and jetsam, with no real anchor in her life now that her husband lived with another woman. She'd never been a woman interested in joining clubs. That was for her close friends and family.

Taking her date calendar out of her purse, she jotted down the telephone number listed as the contact person, someone named Agnes Taylor.

She thought she should at least see what the group had to offer. Perhaps she might learn something helpful. She admitted to herself that she *was* lonely, missed her children, and, yes, missed Don more and more each day. And God knows her nights were almost unbearable. There seemed to be no part of the house in which she could find peace. Don was gone, but his unseen presence seemed to permeate the house. She had become a night owl and had taken to wandering from room to room, from bedroom to kitchen, from kitchen to family room. Sleep would elude her until the wee hours of the night, and the next day she would, of course, be physically tired, emotionally exhausted. Perhaps other women in the same boat could describe what it takes to move forward after divorce.

So a few day later Leanne took her first big step and called Agnes Taylor.

Agnes Taylor sounded cheerful and optimistic when she answered the phone.

"My name is Leanne Matthews and I've been divorced for almost a year. I saw your notice about your support group from the library's bulletin board. Could you tell me a little about . . ."

"Yes, Leanne . . . you don't mind me calling you Leanne?"

"Not at all, please do."

"And I'm Agnes. First, let me tell you that I divorced my husband after forty-five years of marriage."

"Twenty-five years for me."

"I'm sorry, Leanne. Know what you are going through. I think meeting with the group will be helpful."

"This is Leanne Matthews, everyone," Agnes said. "Please introduce yourselves."

"My name is Grace. I am a first wife, and I've been divorced for ten years."

The woman seated next to her said, "My name is Anna. I am a first wife, and I've been divorced for three years."

As the introductions continued, Leanne listened. She learned that some of the women were recently divorced as she was and others who had been divorced for more than fifteen years. *There must be something they get from this support group that keeps them coming.*

Agnes asked Leanne, "Do you drink coffee, or would you prefer a cup of tea?"

"Coffee, black, would be great. And those blueberry muffins over there look to die for."

"You've got it!"

Agnes went over to a small table on which were carafes of hot water for tea and coffee. She soon returned with the coffee, a large muffin, napkins and a fork.

"Enjoy, my dear."

"Thank you very much."

"You're quite welcome," Agnes told Leanne, then took her seat at the head of the table.

"Ladies," Agnes started, "as we all know, 'doing well is the best revenge.' And to make a good, meaningful life for one's self is what each of us is seeking."

Most of the women nodded their heads in agreement.

"Leanne," Agnes continued, "as I told you on the phone, I divorced my husband after forty-five years of marriage. You want to know why? I just didn't want to live with the man anymore. There was nothing in our marriage. It had just dried up, had no life in it, no reason to keep on trying. I couldn't see spending my life trying to breathe life into it."

A woman at the opposite end of the table asked, "What about your children?"

Agnes laughed. "My children were not stupid, not at all. They said it was 'about time.' Not that they didn't love their father. It was because there was always such a miserable atmosphere in our home when they were growing up. They were relieved when we divorced."

As Leanne sipped her coffee and munched on her muffin, she looked around at the women, each of whom had her own divorce story. Most were very well dressed, well groomed, and she was surprised to see several white women among them. Well, she thought, divorce is non-racial.

Later, after she had attended several sessions, one of the women came up and introduced herself.

"Hello, Leanne. My name is Tina Lambeth. I'm glad you've joined us and I want to tell you that being in this group of women has given me more support and courage from my own family."

Leanne had thanked Tina and said she hoped she, too, would find the strength to find new paths in her own life.

But at this first meeting, after listening to the women, it seemed to her that unlike her experience, many in the group had initiated their divorce. Only one or two, like her, had been divorced because of unfaithful husbands.

Everly Babcock, a middle-aged woman, had lost her husband to a younger woman. Her husband, a computer expert, had been sent by his company on a six-month assignment to an island in the Caribbean. He asked Everly for a divorce when he returned home, saying he loved another woman.

Leanne listened intently as Everly described the circumstances of her divorce, the only sign of her dismay being the way she moved her empty coffee cup around in tiny circles.

"We had never had a fight. We always trusted each other. But, well, maybe it was being so far from home for so long . . . but now that I think about it, he was probably just another weak man buckling when this woman undertook a very serious campaign to snag him."

"What's he doing now?" Leanne asked.

"He left the computer company. Last I heard, he and his new wife were running a bed and breakfast on the island. The new wife might have thought he would bring her to the states, but I think he just couldn't face his family and friends and co-workers. He turned into something different. A different person altogether."

Leanne wondered if something similar had happened to Don. She did not know this Alisha Morton, but she couldn't help wondering if this intruder in their lives had somehow changed Don into something different from the man she had married twenty-five years ago.

CHAPTER 30

Macy's was having a sale and Leanne decided it would be a good time to update her fall wardrobe.

She hadn't shopped for clothes since that New York weekend with Don. That long ago weekend when she thought that she and Don were on the same wavelengths of love. *How wrong she was.* And then there was her weight loss. Not a whole lot, but enough for her to notice some of her slacks and skirts were not fitting well at all.

It was ten-thirty, and the store had already been open for a half hour, so it was not crowded. She'd been wearing a size twelve, but decided to check to see if eight would be a better fit, so she headed over to that department. Halfheartedly, she looked through the racks and spotted a mandarin-collar, boiled wool jacket. It was paired with stretch polyester fabric slacks. She already owned a crisp white blouse that she figured would pair up nicely. She picked up a camel-colored wool flannel skirt styled with a side-elastic waist and side seam pockets. She found a candy-red, silk, long-sleeved blouse to wear with the skirt. She was pleased to find a tweed jacket.

She was heading for the dressing rooms when she heard someone call out, "Leanne! Leanne!" Startled, she turned to face Tina Lambeth, a member of the First Wives group.

"Tina! What are you doing here?" Leanne asked.

"I'm the manager of this department, women's clothing."

"Gosh, no wonder you always look so well turned out."

Tina reached for the armful of clothing. "Here, let me take these. You've made some great selections," she said as she accompanied Leanne to the dressing room area and hung the garments on the wall hooks.

"Now, Leanne, if you need any help, I'll be close by, just call." And she said in a quiet voice, "You can use my employee discount."

"Oh, no, Tina, you don't have to do that!"

"Why not?" Tina asked. "We're friends, aren't we? I can use my discount as I please, and I would be so pleased to help you. After all, we're sisters under the skin, aren't we?"

"If you mean because of our divorce experiences, I guess you're right, Tina."

"That's right! Now sing out when you're ready. Have you had lunch yet?"

"No."

"Well, why don't we hop over to the Ninety-Nine?"

"Sounds fine to me. I do have a one-thirty appointment to show a house."

In short order, Leanne tried on her selections and decided to purchase all of them, thanks to Tina's employee discount.

While waiting for Tina, Leanne sat in the shopping mall on a bench facing the entry to Macy's. She phoned the restaurant to say that she was on her way for lunch with a friend. She described herself and gave instructions that she was to be given the lunch check. She felt it was the least she could do, considering the generous discount Tina had given her.

It was a little before noon when they arrived at the restaurant. Leanne was able to find a parking spot very close to the front door. She'd insisted on using her car for the short trip.

As soon as they were seated in a comfortable booth, a server who introduced herself as Joan came to take their order.

"And I'm Mrs. Matthews," Leanne said, alerting the server that she was to get the check.

A few minutes after each checked the menu, they both decided on soup and a sandwich. While waiting for their food, Leanne thanked Tina again for allowing her to use her employee discount.

"Lee, I was happy to do it. It's one of the nice things about my job. Think nothing of it."

"It's much appreciated."

"I've done the same for some of the other First Wives."

"That's wonderful. We women need all the support we can get. Tell me, Tina, if you don't mind, what happened in *your* divorce situation? You're so young."

Tina, shaking her head, tossed her long blonde hair back. Her face took on a sober look and she took a sip of water before she answered.

"It came as a complete shock to me, Leanne. Gene and I met, believe it or not, at a football game. Two of my brothers were playing on teams opposite each other and I was cheering for each team. Naturally I couldn't choose one over the other, although I sort of hoped my older brother would win, figuring my younger brother, a freshman, would have more years to prove himself.

"Sitting beside me, Gene laughed at me all through the game, and after it was over my older brother's team won. He invited me to have dinner at a very elegant restaurant. We hit it off from the start. He was a lawyer and worked as an assistant district attorney, had graduated from Harvard Law School, which I have to tell you really impressed me. I was getting my degree in business management, but it did not take long before I knew I was in love with this delightful, handsome young man. Think of Paul Newman, God rest his soul. My wonderful Gene could have been his double."

"So, you two got married?"

"We did. Happiest day of my life."

"What happened?"

"After a few months he decided he didn't want to be married to me."

"But why?"

"Simple. I wanted to start a family and he didn't."

"Did he say why?"

"Said he didn't want to bring children into this crazy world, the war, terrorists, the failing economy. But the funny thing is he was always ready for sex."

"That sounds odd."

"I thought so, too, but he was adamant that I should not get pregnant. He said that if I did, he would leave.

That's when I told *him* to 'hit the road.' And the next day I filed for a divorce, citing irreconcilable differences."

"I'm so sorry," Leanne said just as the server brought their soup and turkey club sandwiches.

Tina picked up her spoon and waved it in front of Leanne's face, her eyes intense as she continued her sad story of divorce.

"The strangest thing is that six months after our divorce was final, the bastard took up with another woman and she is six months pregnant! Go figure!"

"I can't, Tina. Must have been hard on you."

"It was, mainly because I thought he loved me. How could he reject me for someone else?"

Leanne shook her head, picked up a quarter of her club sandwich, looked over at her friend.

"You know, Tina, I think that there are some men who don't know *what* they want. Some psychologists think that the male of the species wants to ensure his immortality by passing his genes along to the next generation. But there are others who do not have the same focus. They want to be lord and master, control their female partner, even denying *her* the opportunity to reproduce. From what you tell me, my dear, Gene was using you. Good thing you got out when you did."

She took a bite of her sandwich and chewed slowly as Tina nodded.

"You could be right, you know. I never thought about it in that way, but if true, it says to me that Gene just did not love me. What about you?"

Leanne nibbled on a dill pickle before answering.

"Tina, to be truthful, I take some responsibility for what happened. We'd been married for twenty-five years and I . . . well, really, each of us was comfortable with our lives. Don's medical practice was doing well. My real estate business was doing well, too. Our two children were both in college and everything seemed perfect. But now, as I look back on it, I never thought that my husband would ever *look* at another woman! Guess I never figured that if a woman wants a man, she will leave no stone unturned to get him.

"Don and I were not as sexually active as in our earlier years, and I guess we both thought that was normal. I was wrong, very wrong not to understand my husband's needs. And when *that* woman chased him, he asked for a divorce so he could marry her. Looking back on it now, I think his ego was boosted by the fact that he was still able to produce a child. I tell you, it was a painful experience for me!"

CHAPTER 31

Taking care of Jay proved to be much easier than Don had anticipated, mainly because the child was so delightful.

Don had moved the baby's crib into the master bedroom, and when he woke up the next morning, looking over at the smiling baby playing with one of his squeaky toys, he thought, *He's growing up so fast!*

He got out of bed, wondering what he should do first. There was the problem of caring for the child or meeting his own needs. What to do?

He took Jay out of his crib, strapped him into his stroller, gave him a pacifier and wheeled him into the bathroom.

He took a quick shower, shaved and dressed. He then took the baby back to the bedroom, and using a face cloth that he had moistened with warm water, he cleaned, powdered and dressed him in clean clothing.

"Now, my man, let's get us something to eat."

He warmed up a jar of baby cereal and a jar of applesauce that he took from a kitchen cabinet. He put Jay into his high chair and tied a bib around his neck as the child pounded both fists on the tray table

"Ready to eat? Here we go!"

Glancing at his watch to check the time, he saw that it was nearly eight and he still had time to drop Jay off at the day care center and be at his office by nine.

He had a lot to deal with, and his mind bounced from one problem to another. What news might he receive from Alisha? Had her mother been found . . . and in what condition? How to resolve his marriage situation as quickly as possible? What legal responsibilities did he have to Jay? It was almost too much for him to think about. And then there was always his duties to his patients and . . . his staff. Sometime today he would call Frank, his lawyer. God, what an unbelievable mess!

He decided not to eat breakfast but to wait until his coffee break. He did gulp a small glass of orange juice before heading out the door.

At the day care center he informed the day care director, Mrs. Rosa Fallon, that his wife had been called away due to a family emergency. She expressed her sympathy, and when he told her that he hoped she would be able to meet Jay's needs, particularly if he had emergencies regarding patients, he assured her that he would compensate her for any extra hours.

"No problem, Dr. Matthews. He's a lovely child, a joy to take care of.

He thanked her and hurried to the elevator that would take him to his office. He was happy to be in his office, in a familiar serene setting where the only problems he faced were ones he could resolve medically. *I'll take care of personal problems at home, not here.*

He found an e-mail from Alisha when he got home later that day—*Mother hospitalized, serious condition, prognosis poor. Will call after eight. Alisha.*

He had just put the baby to bed when his bedside phone rang. He sat on the bed and picked up the phone.

"Yes, Alisha, how are things going?"

"The police found Mother sitting on a park bench about a mile from our house. Evidently she had been there for two days. People passed right by her." Her voice cracked.

"How is she doing now?"

"You know . . . IV fluids, a ventilator, not aware of anything, comatose, and the doctors say the prognosis is poor."

"I'm very sorry. I know this is hard for your father."

"He's beside himself."

"I can imagine. So I expect you don't know when you are coming home."

"I'm not coming back!"

"What do you mean, 'not coming back'?"

"You want a divorce, don't you?" she fairly shouted over the phone.

He found himself shouting back. "Alisha! You deceived me! Of course I want out! I want a divorce!"

"Well, you can have it!"

"What about Jay?"

"What do you mean, 'what about Jay!' "

Don almost choked on his words. "He's *your* son!"

"I don't want to be a single mother!" she yelled back.

"You're his mother, for God's sake! He's your son," Don hotly reminded her.

"I just told you I *don't* want to be a single mother. Your name is on his birth certificate as his legal father!"

"You're crazy!" he shouted back over the phone.

Her voice was calm, cold, and matter-of-fact when she answered.

"I've already spoken to my lawyer and he said that with a divorce I can give up custody of the child. My focus now is my parents. *They* need me."

"You, you would do that? Deny a child that *you* brought into this world!"

His brain reeled with the undeniable knowledge that this woman was a true certifiable psychopath, a person who saw no right or wrong in pursuing whatever it was that she wanted or thought she wanted. He could barely control his fury.

"Alisha, you deceived me about your pregnancy. You lied about having Japanese ancestry. And now you are dropping off *your* son like a bag of dirty clothes. You are one amoral, crazy bitch!"

He hung up, afraid that if he did not, he would begin to sound incoherent. His mind spun with disbelief.

Sitting on the bed, he assigned major blame to himself. *I have to accept blame for this mess. It was my ego, inflated by sex with a younger woman, seduced by her attention. The weakness was mine, and I will have to pay for that.*

The reminder came to Don's office a week later. Having been busy juggling his practice with caring for the child, he had almost forgotten the prior commitment he had made to serve as chairman for a two-day conference to be held in Philadelphia, about six weeks away. The topic was, ironically, *Advances in the Treatment of Alzheimer's Disease.*

He had to go. He would lose all credibility in his medical association if he did not fulfill this obligation.

What about the baby? he thought. *Thank God Jay was already enrolled in day care, but now what about nights? Who could take a baby who needed care at night?* He thought about his staff, but each one had family responsibilities of her own. Who . . . who could he get to help him? He remembered Mrs. Sparks, but she was out of town.

Before he could stop himself, he dialed a familiar number.

"Hello?"

"Leanne, it's me."

"Don! My God, what's wrong? Are you sick? You sound . . ."

"Leanne, Leanne, oh, my God, I have no right to call you after what I've put you and the children through. I can never, ever tell you how sorry I am." His voice cracking as he struggled to continue.

Leanne interrupted him, "What's wrong? Are you sick?"

"No, no, I'm, I'm okay. But Alisha has left me."

"Left you? When? Where did she go?"

"Ten days ago. She went home to Pittsburgh. Her mother has Alzheimer's, disappeared from home. Police found her. She's in the hospital, not doing well. Her prognosis is poor."

"Don," Leanne's voice was firm and controlled when she broke in with her question. "Don, why are you calling me?"

"I—I need you."

"For what?"

"Please, Leanne, I know I'm asking a lot and . . . I have no right to do so, but I'm in an awful mess!"

"Tell me, Don. Tell me what you want."

"It's such a long story."

"Begin at the beginning."

She heard him take a long, drawn-out breath as if gathering the strength to continue.

"I sent pictures of the baby to Curtis and Jane. Have you seen them?"

"Yes, I have Don. A handsome child."

"Then probably you noticed that he didn't resemble our two kids."

"To be truthful, I did think he had an exotic look, as if he were part something else . . . and I thought he was a very cute baby."

"He is a lovely, healthy baby. But, Leanne, he is *not* my child!"

"What are you talking about?"

"I asked Alisha about his features and she claimed that she had a Japanese grandfather. That information did not sit well with me, so I had a DNA test done that proves I am not the father."

"How can that be?" Leanne asked. "I know that you two were . . ." she paused, founding it difficult to say *sexually active*, so she ended with, "were very close."

"You won't believe this," Don said, "but that . . . I hate to say it, but I was such an idiot. But that conniver was out to get me any way that she could, and I was so dumb, lost all reason and believed her when she said she was pregnant with *my* child."

"What did she say when you told her what the test showed?"

"She had used a sperm donor."

"Oh, my God, Don! She's crazy!"

"Tell me about it! She blurted out that she loved me and this was her desperate attempt to get me."

"Now what, Don?"

"Wouldn't you know it, we were in the middle of this mess when the phone rang. I thought it might be a patient emergency, but it was her father calling about her mother. Naturally she rushed home. She called me last night to say she's *not* coming back, will not contest the divorce, and she is giving up all rights to and responsibilities for the baby."

"She can do that?"

"Apparently she can. I checked with Frank Jones, my lawyer, and he said it's called emancipation of a minor child."

"Don, as angry and hurt as I have been over our divorce, I am sorry that you have been involved in such a sordid affair."

"It was all my stupidity," he insisted, but Leanne tried to reassure him.

"What has happened is in the past, Don, and cannot be changed. Today is a new day. What can I do to help?"

Grateful for Leanne's understanding and lack of bitterness, he forged ahead and explained his problem.

After he explained that he needed to be in Philadelphia for a medical symposium, she agreed to help him.

"I'll be away for two nights. Jay is in day care at my office building . . ."

"Oh, that's where Rosa Fallon works."

"You know her? The director?"

"We served together on the vestry board at church."

"Great! I'll give her your name, address and phone number as the responsible person for the baby. Leanne, how can I thank you?"

"No need, Don. We do have a history together."

CHAPTER 32

Relieved by Leanne's willingness to help him, Don breathed a sigh of relief. He placed an order with a rental company to send a crib with mattress, a high chair, playpen and walker to Leanne's home. He had located her new address when he had gone online to get her telephone number listed with her real estate agency.

He had planned his departure to Philadelphia for a Sunday afternoon flight, and Leanne had said that he could drop Jay off early that afternoon on his way to the airport.

He had purchased a cooler for the jars of baby food, crackers that the child liked, as well as a few of his favorite toys.

He placed a few sets of shirts, coveralls, a pair of shoes and some socks, along with toilet articles into a small overnight bag. He included pj's, three packages of diapers, plus baby wipes. He bought milk and apple juice on his way to Leanne's Sunday afternoon. He made an addition to the list, car seat, that he'd have to leave with Leanne.

It was a pleasant, sunny day when he arrived at Leanne's home that afternoon. She opened the door almost as soon as he got to the front door, an excited wiggling baby in his arms.

"Leanne!"

"Hi, Don. Give him to me!" she said as she reached for the chubby, smiling baby.

"My, he's an armful!" she said as she took the child.

Don agreed. "He is that. But, Leanne, don't you look great!"

"You think so?" she smiled over her shoulder as she walked into the living room with the baby.

"My goodness, you've lost some weight, and it looks good on you! And your hair, I like the way you're wearing it, soft around your face. You look like a young . . ."

"Don't say it, Don," she said and laughed. "You know my age." She turned to the baby. "Well, how are *you*, young man?"

Jay gave her a bubbly, wet, toothless smile.

"I think he's beginning to teethe," Don observed, wiping the baby's drool away with a tissue.

"Let me bring in his things. Did the rental company deliver . . ."

"Everything came and is all set up. Not to worry," she reassured him.

He brought in the supplies he had put together for Jay, as well as the car seat. He and Leanne talked a few minutes about their children, and Don said how much he regretted not being more closely involved in their present lives.

"That may change, Don. You never know, as the saying goes. Keep hope alive!"

"What else can I do?"

"Just be patient."

As he drove to the airport he thought, *How could I have been such a jackass? What I lost was unimaginable. Can I ever get it back?*

Greene Airport in Providence was a user-friendly facility familiar to Don, and he had no difficulty finding a parking space to leave his car. He had a nonstop flight to the city of Brotherly Love and was relieved to be able to get a taxi to his hotel.

He hoped that the two days of the conference would be successful. If nothing else, it would remove him from the painful site of the horrible crisis in his personal life. One thing he knew for certain, the change would give him peace of mind, a feeling he needed. What was in Jay's future? That bothered him the most as he realized, like it or not, he had already bonded with the child.

One thing he knew, he had to put a call in to Frank Jones. The lawyer would help him file for an annulment or divorce, and also help him with Jay's adoption. He hated to think of it, but adoption seemed the only way out. There was no way he could care for a child.

As soon as he reached his hotel room, he put in a call to Leanne.

"Any problems?" He was very anxious about the burden he had placed on her.

"Are you kidding?" she laughed over the phone. "What a delightful child! He's a pleasure to care for, so easy. We're doing fine. Not to worry."

"I'm going to give you the number here at the hotel. You do have my cell number, don't you?"

"Don, don't worry. All systems are go. Relax."

"Good. I should be back Tuesday night. My plane lands at eight, so I should be back by nine."

"Don, the child will be in bed asleep. You can plan to stay over. You can use Curtis's room."

"But won't that be an imposition?"

"Not at all. As a matter of fact, I think it would be easier for everyone."

He had no difficulty retrieving his car from the parking lot. Within minutes he was on his way to Leanne's house.

She had left the driveway light on, as well as the front door light. And to his surprise, she opened the front door, almost, it seemed, the moment his foot hit the step.

"Let me show you where you'll be staying, get you settled." She led him upstairs to Curtis's room, where he dropped his bag and then to Jane's room nearest to hers, where the baby was sleeping. They both tiptoed into the room, checked to find him sleeping soundly.

"He's always been a good sleeper," Don whispered as they left the room. Leanne nodded in agreement.

"Here's the bathroom," she pointed out as they walked down the hall.

"Here is my master suite, at the end of the hall, but I can hear Jay quite easily if he starts to cry."

"Just let me drop my jacket."

Walking down to the kitchen, Leanne thought how unfazed she was by her ex-husband's presence in the same house. But she also knew full well the marked change her life had undergone. *What now? Where do I go from here?*

She had two set glasses on a silver tray and was getting wine from the refrigerator when Don appeared. He had shed his jacket and tie, and his white shirt was open at the collar. He seemed relaxed and comfortable.

"This is a nice house."

"I like it," she said. "It's just enough for me, especially with the kids away at school. It's not too much for me to handle."

"Good. And the kids, doin' okay? I don't hear much of anything from them. I understand why, of course, but I do care," he said soberly.

"It's been hard for them, but both are level-headed and have accepted the changes in their lives. I'm proud of them."

"I am too, Leanne, and I know that you deserve all the credit for that."

"All I did, Don, was to keep reminding them that you are their father and nothing can ever change that."

"Wish I could . . . change things, that is."

"Don, all we have, any one of us, is this moment. Yesterday is gone and tomorrow is not here. So what we do with the moment we have, that's what matters. I try not to dwell on the past, can't change it, and I attempt to strive for a good future, with the help of the Lord."

He tipped his glass in a salute to her.

"You always were a positive, practical thinker."

"Works for me," she smiled, returning his salute with her own glass of wine.

For a few moments each was quiet, sipping their wine.

Finally Leanne spoke.

"Your conference, was it successful?"

"It was. Some new modalities, new treatments that are being advanced, as well as promising methods of early diagnosis for Alzheimer's were presented."

"There does seem to be quite a bit of public funding for research. So all in all, it was a worthwhile session? I'm glad you could go."

"Thanks, Leanne, for helping me."

"It was a pleasure having such a sweet, lovable child in the house. What do you plan to do if his mother does give him up?"

"I have thought about putting him up for adoption . . . I don't know. The strangest thing, Leanne, is even knowing that he is not my biological child, I've bonded with him. Was there when he was born, cut the cord. I do feel responsible for him."

He poured a little more wine into his glass, questioning Leanne with raised eyebrows, asking her if she wanted a refill.

She shook her head.

"I can imagine how you feel, Don. It is in your nature to be a caring person. That's why you're such a good physician, why your patients love you."

"Kind of you to say that."

"It's true."

She watched him sipping his wine, remembering the many happy times they had shared at the day's end with small talk and wine. Those had been happy, satisfying times, and she realized that despite the anguish and turmoil she had suffered, she wanted that time back. Don was the only man she had ever loved. There would never be another.

CHAPTER 33

"No need to go into it, Don. But I should say that if you gave off any warning signals, I totally missed them, and I regret that—if indeed that was the case. But after twenty-five years of a trouble-free marriage, at least from my viewpoint, I would have sworn in any court that I knew you better than anyone else on earth. But apparently I did not. That is why it came as such a shock and why it left me so devastated."

"No, Leanne," he said, "you are not guilty of anything—even indirectly. I am *completely* to blame here. I was the one who strayed, who allowed myself to be drawn into an action that I *knew* to be wrong, that I *knew* would have dire consequences if it were to come to light."

Watching the expression of both shame and distress on his face, Leanne suddenly had no taste for anymore mea culpa and she waved her hand, indicating he should stop.

"Enough, Don. We both made mistakes . . . enough. It's behind us now." Then she changed the subject. "What are you doing for Thanksgiving?"

"I don't know. So much upheaval in my life. Nothing, I guess."

"Why don't you and Jay come here? The kids will be here."

"You think *they* want to see me?"

"Why not?" she responded quickly. "As I've told them, you are the only father they will ever have. And I, for one, believe it's high time we had some healing in this family!" She rose from her seat, saying, "The house is already locked up. Have a good night. See you in the morning."

"Goodnight, Leanne. Thanks."

"Goodnight, Don. Sleep well."

"I will."

He sat thinking how magnanimous Leanne had been to invite him and Jay to Thanksgiving dinner.

Going up the stairs to her bedroom, Leanne wondered if she had been foolish in offering an opening to a reconciliation. Her heart told her it was what she wanted, but her brain advised caution.

Going in her room, she thought back to their early years. Marriage, getting to really "know" one another, how Don always shaved in the morning in just his pajama bottoms. The way he'd acted the first time she told him he was going to be a father. The look on his face—disbelief, excitement—had thrilled her. He had dropped to his knees, his arms around her knees, his head pressed up against her body, hugging her fiercely.

"Oh, my God, Leanne," he had said, "are you sure?"

"Don, of course I'm sure," she had said, cradling his head in her hands. She had already checked with her doctor and he had confirmed what she had suspected.

Leanne was surprised by how much she missed little Jay. In the few nights that she had cared for him, something about him appealed to her. Maybe it was the knowing that his own mother didn't want him and knowing he did not belong to the only male he saw daily in his young life. She thought back to the love and care she and Don had given to Curtis and Jane.

She recalled the pride she took in seeing them grow and develop into responsible young people. Would having Don and Jay at the holiday dinner table prove to be the beginning of getting her family back again? Or would it further divide them?

The next morning she took care of Jay, bathing and dressing him, feeding him his breakfast. Don took advantage of her help with the baby so he could shower, dress and take Jay's belongings out to his car.

"You've done enough for me, Leanne, and I appreciate it. I'll grab something to eat during my coffee break."

"Not even a cup of coffee?"

"Thanks, I've imposed on your generosity enough."

"Okay, but plan to come for Thanksgiving, Don. Please do it for me."

Leanne had made up her mind that she wanted her family to be whole again, and she was determined to make that happen. Even if she failed, it was worth a try.

She had suggested that Don leave Jay's crib, playpen and high chair at her house until later decisions had been made.

"They are not in the way, and when you come for Thanksgiving they will be here," she had suggested.

So now she was about to "bite the bullet" and call Curtis.

"Hi, Curt, how are you?"

"Hi, Mom. I'm fine. What's up?"

"Nothing much. I'm expecting you and Jane for Thanksgiving. And Bob, too. He's not going out to California, is he?"

"No, he's going for Christmas, to be with his folks."

"I understand. Curtis, I have to ask you to do something for me."

"Sure, Mom. What is it?"

"I know you will say no, but I'm going to ask you anyway."

"Okay, tell me what you want."

"Your father's new wife has left him and the baby. He's getting a divorce . . ."

"My God, Mom, you're not going to take him back!"

"I don't know about that, but I do want to invite him for Thanksgiving."

"No way! No way!" Curtis's voice was tight with anger. His mother heard it and was not surprised.

"Mom! You've been through enough. Look what he put us, put you, through! Total upheaval for the family, all for someone not worth your little finger! No, Mom, I am not going to sit down to eat a Thanksgiving dinner with that man!"

Leanne controlled her fury at her son's outburst, although she understood his anger. She spoke slowly and calmly. "That man, as you call him, is your father. You carry his blood that you will someday pass on to your son, and all your ranting and raving will not change that! I know that you children have been hurt, as I have been, but we all, each one of us, has frailties, flaws, imperfections that influence our lives. Listen to yourself, Curt. And if you do, you will realize that your inability to forgive your father points to your own lack of empathy or sympathy to other people. I don't want that to be a part of who you are.

"As a lawyer, you will be bound to deal with all kinds of human weaknesses. So I'm counting on you to put aside your feelings and come on Thanksgiving. I do understand. I do love you, Curtis. Please, for me, will you come?"

"You're asking a lot, Mom, but I'll come. I love you, too."

"Thank you, son. This means a lot to me."

When she called her daughter, Jane's response was much like her brother's. The same anger, ranting and raving about what Don had done to the family. However, she soon softened a little.

"I do miss Dad. Is he all right?"

When she told Jane that Don's new wife had left him and the baby to help her father take care of her ailing mother, Jane answered, "Just as well that she was out of Dad's life. Mother, since you're doing the Thanksgiving thing, would you mind if I bring a friend?"

"Of course, Jane. You know that's never a problem. Always happy . . ."

"Well, I've been dating this guy . . . kind of want you to check him out."

"Honey, that sounds exciting. Be happy to have him, what's his name?"

"Sam, Sam Adams. He's from Montreal."

"I'll be very happy to meet him. Curtis is bringing his roommate, Bob Sato, along. And, Janey, I have to tell you that your father *is* hurting about what's happened. Please, don't be judgmental. Remember, he's your father, and despite everything he loves you kids, misses you so much."

Jane said something about her mother not taking Don back.

"Jane," Leanne retorted, "I don't know what I'm going to do, but it will be *my* decision, won't it?"

CHAPTER 34

Frank Jones reached Don at his office in the medical building.

"Don," he asked, "have you heard from Alisha?"

"She called a few days ago. Her mother did not survive. The services have been held and she plans to remain in Pittsburgh to care for her father."

"So she is not contesting the divorce?"

"That's what she says, and also that she does not want custody of Jay."

"I have received a sworn statement from her lawyer that addresses those issues. When you can find the time, Don, try to come in so we can start the process."

"Thanks so much, Frank."

Don checked his calendar as soon as he hung up the telephone. He noted that his patient load was light on Thursday and that there were a few patients that could be rescheduled. He really wanted the whole afternoon clear to consult with his lawyer.

He wondered if he should ask Frank about the feasibility of an annulment, as opposed to a no-fault divorce. He had not informed his staff about his personal situation, although they knew his wife was out of town and that Jay was in day care.

He did inform Becky that he would not be in the office Thursday afternoon, that the staff could have the afternoon free. He asked her to reschedule those patients involved.

On Thursday, Don had a quick lunch and was in Frank's office at one o'clock, the appointed time.

"Don, I'm glad you're here. I've cleared my calendar so we will have plenty of time to discuss your issues."

"Great! I'm anxious to get started."

"I know. There are several things to consider. First, even though the DNA test proves you are not the biological father, your name is on the baby's birth certificate as the legal father.

"As for your marriage, it may be deemed to be fraudulent because your wife misled you, lied about the child being yours when she knew she had used a sperm donor.

"Now, if you divorce her, she has declared that she does not wish custody of the child. But still, you can sue her for child support if you choose."

"God, no, Frank! I do not want to have anything, nothing at all to do with that woman! Never! No!"

Noting his client's agitation, Frank responded, "Man, take it easy."

"Just thinking about her upsets me. No, I can support Jay if I have to. Be no problem, none at all."

"Good. I need you to sign some papers stipulating a no-fault divorce on the grounds of incompatibility or irreconcilable differences. I will be forwarding copies of these to her lawyer as well."

"Frank, how *long* will this take? To get the divorce, I mean?"

"Once the decree is handed down, you have to wait sixty days for it to be final."

"Can't come too soon for me."

"How are you managing to take care of the child, Don?"

"It's hard because I have to meet his every need. But he is a pleasant, amiable child. As long as he's fed and clothed, kept clean, he responds to me with a happy grin."

"Think he misses Alisha?"

"Don't know, he doesn't seem to be looking for her, so I don't really know. You know, Frank, when I had to go out of town to a medical meeting, my ex-wife babysat Jay. She said he was the easiest child she had ever taken care of."

"Wonderful. Must have made you feel good."

"It did. We talked some about our differences. I have many, many regrets over my despicable behavior, I have to tell you, but incredibly Leanne said, 'I try not to dwell on the past.' She seems willing to forgive, not that I deserve one iota of forgiveness for what I have done to her and my children. Believe it or not, Frank, she invited me and the baby to Thanksgiving dinner. I expect to have some tense, anxious moments when I face Curtis and Jane. I'm very anxious to know how we will make out."

"Don't forget, you are their father. Just remember that."

"Thanks, Frank. Don't know what I would do without you."

Frank grinned at him. "Wait 'til you get my fee, see how you feel then."

Leanne was not going to tell the children that young Jay was not their father's child, not their half-brother; she would let Don do that. She could only hope that the innocent child, in effect now parentless, would receive their consideration and empathy.

Leanne Matthews was an innately positive person, and she had put a positive spin on her expectations for the day. Of course she expected some initial tensions when the family gathered for the first time in months. But she prayed that would be short-lived.

To save time and conserve her energy, Leanne had a cleaning service to come in and clean the house. The windows sparkled, the furniture gleamed, the rugs were spotless. The house had a fresh, airy, comfortable feel to it.

By late morning, she had already set the table with her best china, silverware and glassware. Arrays of fall flowers were in the center of the table. The precooked turkey, which came with mashed potatoes, gravy and stuffing, had been delivered that morning at eleven. All she had to do was pop it into the oven for an hour or so just before serving it.

Everything was set, but she still gladly accepted Don's offer to come over an hour early to help her. He also said he would be bringing the wine.

"Would you mind carving the turkey?" she asked him.

"Be happy to do it," he said, inwardly wincing as he recalled the many times he had performed that task for his family. But he was determined to put the best possible face on whatever happened that day.

When Leanne opened the front door for Don and Jay, the baby bounced gleefully, obviously recognizing her.

"He knows you!" Don exclaimed.

"Give him to me! How are you doing, big boy?" She kissed his forehead. It was obvious Jay was happy to see her.

"You know, Don, he is a very smart child."

"Seems to be."

"Do you think he'll be okay in the playpen for now? Have to be in the kitchen doing a few things, and you'll want to get started on the turkey. We can move the playpen into the kitchen."

"Sure smells good in here," Don observed. He opened some of the pots, checked the rice, greens, a pot of gravy simmering on a back burner.

"Got sweet potatoes?" he asked and grinned at her.

Laughing, she teased him, "Now what do you think? That I would forget one of your favorites?"

"I know one thing for sure, wouldn't be Thanksgiving without your candied sweet potatoes."

"Don . . ."

Still standing in front of the stove, he turned to look at her. She had been tossing a large bowl of salad greens with silver forks.

"Yes, Leanne?"

"It's good to have you here. I don't know what kind of future we might have, but for me it's almost as if you've been away on a long trip and you've come home. I don't really know . . . except I'm glad you are . . . back."

He did not miss the sober look on her face.

"Leanne," he began moving the few steps from the stove to the table. Facing her, he placed his hand on her right shoulder. It was the first time he had touched her. She welcomed the warmth of his hand.

"Leanne," he said, "I, too, don't know what's ahead for us, but I want you to know how much I appreciate your understanding and support."

"You are most welcome here anytime. By the way, Don, I haven't told the children about the nature of your relationship with Jay. I think you should be the one to explain it?"

"Right. I just hope Curtis and Jane will understand."

"They are sensible children. They will understand, I'm sure. Would you take the turkey out of the oven? Needs to cool down a bit before you carve it."

"No problem," he said, wishing that the rest of this day would have "*no problems.*"

CHAPTER 35

They had placed Jay's playpen in the corner of the kitchen near the door to the dining room. From where he stood near the table, Don could see that the child had turned over and was asleep.

"Look, he's out like a light. Must be the soothing warmth of the kitchen."

"There's a light afghan in the living room. Let me get it to cover him." She returned with a colorful coverlet that she laid over the sleeping baby.

She handed Don a white chef's apron to put on over his gray slacks and blue turtleneck shirt.

"Still hung on to this, huh?"

"Never know, do you, when certain items may come in handy."

He picked up the electric knife and started carving the turkey.

"Curtis will pick Jane up at Simmons College and they will be coming together," she told him. "And I think, from what Jane said on the phone, she might be bringing a special somebody named Sam Adams. Curtis's roommate, Bob, is coming, too. He's a real nice young man . . . came with Curt for dinner a couple of times."

"I'm anxious to see the kids . . . been too long. I've really missed them," Don said as he bent over his task.

Leanne handed him a large serving platter, and he began to arrange turkey slices on it.

"I should leave the drumsticks whole, shouldn't I? Remember how much Curtis always liked them."

"I think you'd better. We sure don't need any extra friction."

"Right."

With all the chores completed, they went into the living room to wait for the guests to arrive.

"Leanne," Don said as he took a seat in a wing chair across from the sofa where Leanne sat. "As we've said before, we don't know what our future holds, but I want you to know that I am filing for a no-fault divorce. Alisha is adamant that she does not want to be a single mother. She does not want custody rights, and has agreed to the baby's adoption."

"I'm sorry that things didn't turn out better for you, Don."

"It's been a costly affair for me, actually for all of us, and I'm to blame! I wish I knew how to right a wrong that can't be undone."

"A day at a time, Don. One day at a time," she urged sincerely, wanting to ease his mind.

Don was again wearing his navy blue blazer. Leanne saw and felt his tension and nervousness. She had never seen him this way. He was still a handsome man, even with the silver streaks in his close-cropped hair. He was strumming the fingers of his left hand on the armrest of the wing chair and frequently glanced at his watch.

"What time did you say the kids will be here?"

"What's the time now?"

He looked at his watch.

"It's one-thirty."

"I told them two o'clock. I thought we could visit a while, sit down to the table at three."

"I know you are apprehensive about seeing the kids, Don. I am, too, but I hope we can present a united front."

A palpable silence fell between the couple. After all, twenty-five years of married life meant that they were all aware of the thoughts and vibes of each other.

Leanne broke the silence.

"I think Boston College and Holy Cross are playing football . . ."

"That's right! Let's check it out."

He picked up the remote from the coffee table and located the game. It had just started.

"Keep it low, Don. Don't want to wake the baby," Leanne cautioned.

He turned the volume down, and she went to see if Jay had been disturbed, came back with an "okay" symbol.

She was just about to sit down when she heard a car in the driveway.

"Don, they're here."

Quickly turning off the television, he said, "Let me open the door."

When Donovan Matthews opened the door and saw his son standing there, he instinctively reached for him, grasping his hand and pulling him over the threshold.

"Curtis! Son, it's great to see you! How are you?"

"Hi, Dad. I'm fine, good to see you, too."

Jane came up right behind her brother. Her grin when she saw her father brought tears to his eyes.

"Janey, baby, I'm so glad to see you!"

Jane hugged her father back because, despite all that had happened, she *was* glad to see him. She turned to greet her mother, who had joined them in the front hall.

"Dad, Mother, I want you to meet my friend, Sam. Sam, these are my parents, Dr. Matthews and my mom, Mrs. Matthews."

Sam extended his hand to Leanne, who gave him a warm smile, shook his hand. "Welcome, Sam Adams."

"Thank you, ma'am."

Then he extended his hand to Don. "Dr. Matthews, my pleasure, sir."

"The pleasure is mine, Sam."

Coats, scarves, and caps were hung on the clothes tree in the front hall.

Curtis introduced Bob to his father, saying, "Dad, this is my roomie at law school, Bob Sato."

"Nice to meet you, sir," Bob said, shaking Don's hand.

"So, you're the guy who is hitting the law books with my son. I'm very happy to meet you."

"This first year is really keeping us up nights, I can tell you that."

"You have a beautiful home, Mrs. Matthews," Sam remarked.

"Thank you, Sam. I like it."

Just then Jane asked, "Sam, would you mind bringing in the dessert that I made? It's on the floor of the front passenger seat."

"No problem," Sam said, and a few moments later returned with a large glass bowl covered with a plastic wrap.

"Look, Mom, it's a chocolate dessert that I made."

"Honey, that was so thoughtful. You know how much I love chocolate," she said, eyeing the layers of whipped cream, devil food's cake, chocolate pudding and crushed candy bars. "This is elegant. I'll put it in the fridge."

"No, I'll do it. You sit down."

Jane left the living room, proceeded through the dining room into the kitchen.

"Mom, there's a baby in here!"

She put the trifle on the counter as everyone rushed into the kitchen.

"He's mine," Don said as he scooped the now wide-awake child up in his arms.

"Yours?" Curtis and Jane spoke in unison.

The baby started to cry, unaccustomed to the strangers surrounding him.

Leanne spoke to Don. "Give him to me, Don. He needs to be changed."

"Thanks, Leanne."

They all moved back into the living room, Curtis and Jane forming a united front as they sat on the sofa, staring intensely at their father across the coffee table.

Curtis could barely contain himself.

"You mean that kid is our half-brother?"

Don heard the anger and dismay in his son's voice and saw the cold disbelief in his eyes.

"Believe it or not, up to a month ago I *thought* he was."

206

"What do you mean, *thought he was*? You married that . . . that woman who said you got her pregnant, didn't you?"

No one noticed that Bob and Sam had quietly retreated into the kitchen, Bob having motioned to Sam as soon as they realized that a family confrontation was under way.

"Their parents are divorced," Bob confided to Sam. "Not sure, but from what Curt has said, a younger woman was involved . . . and a baby."

"Jane told me a little, too. I think both she and her brother have been really angry at their father, but something tells me the parents might get back together. Don't really know, but why else this Thanksgiving dinner?" Sam wondered.

"Who knows?" Bob said.

Donovan Matthews, M.D., recognized that facing his children at this moment demanded that he summon every bit of courage and sincerity that he could possibly manage.

He could not remember ever being in a more difficult situation. How to make Curtis and Jane understand? These two *were* his children, blood of his blood, bone of his bone, and half of their genes were from him. He *had* to make them see him as the father who loved them always, despite *his* weaknesses.

Curtis glared at him, as if daring him to explain. Jane was twisting a curl of her dark brown hair, something she had always done when upset.

How could he explain his behavior that had so disrupted their lives? Despite endless soul-searching and self-analysis, he himself could not understand it.

He sat looking at their silent accusing faces. Before he could try to explain, Leanne came back into the living room with the changed, smiling, happy baby in her arms.

Curtis felt a twinge of jealousy as he watched his mother interacting with Jay. *What is she doing with a baby? My mother!*

Leanne saw her son's look of disapproval, but chose not to acknowledge it. Instead she spoke tò Don.

"I'm going to feed him now so that he will be comfortable when we all sit down to eat."

"Thanks, Leanne, that would be great."

When she left, he launched right into what amounted to a confession. "I lost a wonderful woman when I betrayed your mother. I was stupid, selfish, and flattered by the attention of a young woman. And I will live with that regret until the day I die. But I do need to explain what happened. Anyway, Alisha told me . . . believe me," he shook his head, "this is hard. When she told me she was pregnant with my child, I did not believe her, not at all! I thought I had been careful, but . . . well, you know what happened.

"When Jay was born, Alisha rejected him at first, and I thought that was strange and troublesome. The next day she seemed to accept him. However, I was concerned because he did not look at all like you kids. I expected some difference, but I also expected some similarities, too. She said the differences were probably due to an

Asian relative in her family, but still I was suspicious. Finally I had a DNA test done which proved I am not the father . . . ."

"But, Dad," Jane interrupted, "who is?"

Don was reluctant to be more specific, but knew he had no choice.

"I don't know. She confessed to using a sperm donor . . ."

Curtis jumped up. "Bob, Bob, get in here! You have to hear this!"

Bob and Sam rushed in.

"What is it?" Bob asked.

"Dad has been telling us about Jay. His mother used a sperm donor and lied, told Dad the baby was his! DNA test said 'no way'!"

Curtis turned to his father, barely able to contain his excitement."Dad! Bob has been a sperm donor, paid for his college . . ."

"You, Bob?"

"Yes, sir, I did, and I have to tell you something. When I first saw Jay, I was shocked because he looked so much like my younger brother, Morris. I couldn't believe it! Here, wait a minute, I have a picture in my wallet."

He pulled out a snapshot of three boys, ages perhaps four, six and eight. He showed the picture to Don. "That's me, with Caleb on my left and Morris in front of us."

"I'll be damned!" Don said, "There *is* a strong resemblance!"

He called to Leanne, "Leanne, you've got to see this."

He showed her the photo. "Do you see a resemblance between Jay and Bob?"

She looked at the photograph of the three Sato brothers, looked again at Bob, who was smiling the same smile that Jay had. "They look very much alike, all of them. Almost as if from the same family."

"You are right. Leanne, Bob is a sperm donor and Jay was conceived by a sperm donation. What are the odds that Jay could be Bob's son?"

Excitement over the possibility of Jay's being Bob's son had the effect of releasing tension for everyone.

Bob asked Leanne, "May I hold him for a minute?"

Everyone laughed when the baby went to Bob. "It's almost like he knows you," Leanne said.

"Dr. Matthews, would a DNA test prove that he is my son?" Bob asked.

"Well, DNA was what proved I was not the father."

"I want to do it. Can you help me?"

"Can you meet me at my office tomorrow?"

"Sure can! Thanksgiving holiday, you know . . . no classes."

"Come any time and we'll start the ball rolling."

When they sat down to eat, Don insisted on saying grace, in which he thanked God for "all blessings." There was an echo of "Amen" from everyone.

Leanne looked around her Thanksgiving table with the profound hope that her family would flourish and find happiness once again.

An innocent baby was the catalyst. Who knew?

CHAPTER 36

The test came back. Bob picked up the envelope, along with the rest of the mail, both his and Curtis's. He made himself sit down at his desk in his room, sort his mail from his roommate's, and then turn the envelope around several times, almost afraid to open it. He wanted to share the moment with someone, but it was *his* life that would be most affected by the truth inside the envelope. What if he *were* Jay's father? How would his *folks* react to finding out they had a grandson?

At that fateful Thanksgiving dinner Dr. Matthews had said that it was his intention to allow Jay to be adopted, that he was in the process of getting a divorce, and at his age he did not believe he could care for Jay.

Bob wondered what legalities he would face as a single parent himself if he tried to adopt the child. He could bear the suspense no longer. He reached for a letter opener and was about to slide it through the envelope flap when he heard Curtis's footsteps on the back stairs of their apartment.

When Curtis opened the door, Bob came rushing out from his room, waving the brown envelope.

"You are just in time, my man! In this envelope lies my *future*."

"You got the results? Yes or no?"

"About to find out now."

He pulled a white sheet of paper out and read silently while Curtis watched Bob's face. When he realized that Bob's eyes were becoming wider and wider as he came to the conclusion at the bottom of the page, Curtis said, "Well, tell me!"

Bob grinned.

"Jay is *my* son."

Overcome with emotion, he sat down at the kitchen table. "I need to call your father. Think that would be all right?"

"Of course." Curtis glanced at his watch. "It's probably a good time, six-thirty."

He pulled his cell phone from his pocket. "I'll get him for you."

He dialed the number, gave the cell phone to Bob.

"Dr. Matthews, Bob Sato here. The news came today. I am Jay's father."

Responding to Don's congratulations, Bob said, "Thank you very much. And I surely appreciate any help you can give me. Yes, sir, I'll be in touch. Thanks again for everything."

Bob looked over at Curtis. "Your father congratulated me but said there were some legal issues I will have to consider. He said I will need legal counsel to guide me in claiming Jay as my son. He is going to help me. I don't suppose my standing as a first-year law student will have any effect."

"You never know," Curtis replied, trying to sound encouraging.

Don met with Frank Jones and told him that the DNA test proved that Bob Sato was Jay's biological father.

"And does he want to adopt him?"

"Yes, Frank, he does. What kinds of legal problems will he have to face?"

"He should, of course, have a lawyer, and a family court will expect the lawyer to look after what's best for the minor child."

"That makes sense to me. And Frank, Bob told me that he called his parents in California and they were thrilled."

Frank nodded.

"That is good to hear, and I do believe that with the DNA results, Bob should be in a position to adopt. Should not be a problem."

"Good. I do care about Jay and want the best for him. Bob seems to be well-grounded, and I think he will no doubt become a fine lawyer. Any judge will see that as a professional, he will be able to support his son. And it is good that he has his family's support."

"Agreed. Now Don, as far as your divorce is concerned, progress is being made. Documents I have received from Alisha's lawyer indicate that she is not contesting the divorce, seeks no alimony, and is agreeable to the child's adoption and doesn't want shared custody. And Don, I see no reason to tell her that the child's biological father has been found, because per rules of the sperm bank, donors are not identified unless they sign a document that they wish to be known."

"That should bode well for Bob. He does not need any extra problems. He has already asked me and Leanne to be godparents."

"Really? How does your ex-wife feel about that?"

"Frank, she's pleased. When she was Jay's babysitter when I went to Philly, she really bonded with him. Man, I have to tell you that I have hopes that someday, somehow, I may get my family back. Am I being foolish or premature thinking such a thing may happen? I'm almost afraid . . ."

"Listen, my friend, there should always be hope. Stranger things have happened. Both of you are good people, and I, for one, believe that things will work out for you."

"Leanne, this is Don. How are you?"

"I'm just fine, Don. What's up?"

"I had to call to let you know how much I appreciate what you did."

"What did I do?"

"You brought us together on Thanksgiving. Who knew what was going to happen that day? What were the chances that . . . that Jay's real father would be revealed?"

His response was sober and clearly deeply felt, and it struck Leanne as completely genuine.

"I, for one, have learned a whole lot about myself. As a physician I am used to making considered decisions. I cannot recall a time when I gave a patient casual or questionable advice. But on a personal level, I had no inkling that I could be as weak and as vulnerable as the next man. I never thought that I was capable of behavior that would be so disastrous, causing so much pain and disruption in our lives. Fact is, I *wasn't* thinking, certainly not with my full faculties. Can you . . . will you . . . forgive me?"

"Oh, Don, as I told you, the past is just that, past, and we can't change what has already happened. And as for forgiveness, consider it done. Remember, the fault was not all yours. It takes two to keep a marriage healthy."

"You are a saint."

"No, I'm not! I have many imperfections, you know that."

"Stay well, Leanne."

"You do the same, Don."

As she hung up the telephone, Leanne felt a surge of hope.

God willing, I might get my family back.

CHAPTER 37

Bob was elated with the news that he was a father, and his smiling face told it all.

He told Curtis, "Even though it wasn't something I had ever given thought to when I was donating, somehow knowing that a human being is alive in this world because of me, and that I've actually met him, is an awesome feeling."

"Hard to believe, isn't it?"

"You're telling me! Man, I want to tell you it was one lucky day for me when we met! Who knew my life would change so much. And your mother, without knowing it, *she* brought me and my son together. It's almost as if the stars were aligned. Like it was meant to be."

"And your parents? What did they say?"

"Can't wait! I'm so glad they will be coming east to visit. My brothers are glad, too. It will be great to have my family together again." Then he stopped speaking, his face red. "Oh, man, I shouldn't have said that, knowing your family . . ."

"It's all right, Bob. I've always loved my dad, and I do want him back in my life. My mother talked to me about my relationship with him. She told me that if I couldn't forgive him . . ." Curtis's voice faltered a bit, but he continued, "She said if I couldn't understand his 'slip and fall,' so to speak, then I was not a compassionate human being. Not one of us is perfect. We all have shortcomings," she said.

"I consider my mother a remarkable woman. She was the one most sorely devastated by what happened. I guess I have to try to be the man she wants me to be."

Curtis rose from his seat at the kitchen table of their apartment and got a beer from the refrigerator. He raised his eyebrows to ask Bob if he wanted one, but Bob declined.

Curtis open his can of beer, swallowed, resumed his seat and continued to talk.

"Bob, I want my family back together, too. I may never understand why my dad did what he did. But he is my *dad*." He took another swallow before continuing. "The only one I'll ever have, and I do want him back in my life. I miss him."

"I know, Curt, I know. Maybe you should tell him what you've just told me."

"Maybe you're right."

"I think I am. He'll never know unless he hears it from you. And Curtis, for my money, your dad is one upright guy. I'm grateful for the help he's given me."

When Curtis told Bob how he missed his dad, his memory peeled back to his younger days, his father helping him with his homework, always encouraging him to do his best, be it school, sports, learning to ride his first bike, or learning to swim, something Curtis really excelled at.

And he could always talk to his father. Perhaps, he thought, that was what he missed most. He had not been able to share his law school experiences with him. And the gulf between them seemed to be widening.

Curtis Matthews was taller than his father by about two inches. He had the slim, sleek body of a swimmer. Kept his hair close-cropped, had piercing dark brown eyes beneath bold, black eyebrows. With high, well-defined cheekbones, he was a striking young man.

Becky was surprised when he appeared at her desk, asking if he could see Dr. Matthews.

"I'm Curtis Matthews, his son. It's not urgent, I don't want to upset him," he explained.

"He's with a patient now, but I'll let him know you're here. Please, have a seat," Becky said checking the roster.

As he waited, his eyes fell on a news magazine that had the new president-elect on its cover. *This man lost his father. Mine is in a nearby office, and I can and will talk to him.*

A few minutes later Becky told Curtis his father was free and he should follow her.

She led him past a row of closed examining rooms to an office at the end of the corridor. DONOVAN MATTHEWS, MD was printed in gold letters on the door.

Curtis had been at his dad's old office, but had never been in this one at the medical association. He was impressed.

Becky knocked on the door.

"Come in, come in!"

Don opened the door and pulled his oldest child into a bear hug.

"Curtis! So glad to see you. Come in! Thanks, Becky," he said, following Curtis inside.

Closing the door, he asked, "Are you all right, son?"

"Dad, I'm fine."

"Everything good at law school?"

"Oh, yes. I'm knee-deep in torts, felonies, crimes and wrongdoings. But it's interesting stuff, and I'm in a great study group along with Bob, so we're hanging in there."

"Good. I know you will make a fine lawyer."

"Thanks, Dad. Look, I know you are busy, but . . ." He paused, but then pressed on. "I just want you to know that I really do care about you, want the best for you. I mean, I miss you and want you back in my life. Being in law school has helped me better understand a little of how unwanted and unplanned problems can come up in life, anyone's life. Dad, I know Mom still loves you and so do I, and Jane, too."

Tears streamed down Don's cheeks as he listened to expressions of love from his firstborn child. His face was red and he felt his heart racing.

"Curt, how . . . how can you forgive me? I turned my back on you and the family I loved, not giving a minute's thought to the havoc I was creating. I realize now that divorce can have an effect on children, no matter what age. I assumed, Lord knows I wasn't thinking, thought you kids would be okay.

I *don't* deserve to have a son like you, Curt. I really don't," Don said, drying his tears. "I have a remarkable son in you, Curt, and I thank the Good Lord for you."

"Well, Dad, you're my *father*, always will be. Don't forget that."

Not wanting to take up too much of his father's day, Curtis soon left, promising to keep in touch, to stay close. Don immediately called Leanne at her office.

"Leanne, thank you for the wonderful kids you have given me."

"Well, thank *you*," she said and laughed. "But you *know* I did not do it alone. So what's up?"

"Curtis came to see me at my office; he just left. Leanne, he told me that he *loves* me, wants me back in his life! How wonderful is that?"

"Don, I can't tell you how happy, how relieved that makes me. It has been quite a struggle for him. I knew he was hurting, and that is why I tried to be patient with him."

"I know that and I can't thank you enough."

"I kept hoping and praying he would be able to come to grips with the situation and see his way to a loving resolution instead of the gloom and doom he had been seeing. My prayers have been answered. Of course, Jane's reactions have never been as extreme as Curt's. She rarely expressed resentment toward you. But then, she has always been a pliant, forgiving child . . ."

"And for that I am grateful. Leanne, uh, doing anything tonight?" he asked hopefully. "I'd love to bring dinner. Bob Sato wants to spend some time with Jay, so he is picking him up for an overnight visit. They seem to be bonding nicely. He'll drop him off at day care in the morning. That has been arranged."

Don stopped at a local grocery store that sold fully prepared meals, selecting a small roasted chicken, a container of gravy, a container of cooked rice and butternut squash.

He selected a salad mix and a half dozen soft rolls. A bottle of sparkling cider caught his eye and he added that to his shopping cart. For dessert, he bought Leanne's favorite butter pecan ice cream.

When he got to her house, he was glad to see her car in the driveway and lights blazing all over the house. He felt welcome.

Indeed, as soon as he approached the front door, Leanne was there opening the door, reaching for the packages.

"Don, good to see you. Let me take some of those."

When he got back to the kitchen, Leanne was already preparing the food on plates to reheat in the microwave. "If you look into that cupboard to your right, Don, you'll find glasses for the cider. Everything looks so good."

"I hope you'll enjoy it. Did you sell the house?"

"The clients liked it very much, and have put in an offer. So we'll see."

Moments later they carried their plates of food into the dining room. Leanne lighted the candles on the table, extinguished the dining room light, and they began to eat.

Don couldn't help himself. He was overcome with emotion. He was with his wife, the woman he now knew that he loved more than anyone in his life. She was his other half, made him feel whole.

He told her about his conversation with Curtis.

"He's a very extraordinary young man. I'm proud to be his father."

"You helped raise him, Don. You always were a big part of his development. He's more like you than you know."

"Thanks for saying that, Leanne."

"It's true."

They finished their meal, put the leftover food away and took their glasses of cider into the living room.

As if it were the most natural thing to do, they sat side by side on the sofa. Leanne took another sip of her sparkling cider, placed her glass on the coffee table.

"So," Leanne asked, "what's new?" She could see and feel that this might be an eventful moment.

"What is it, Don?"

"Today my son and I were united. And today I am a free man. My divorce has become final."

"Oh, my God! Don, it's over?"

"Yes, Leanne, the long nightmare is over."

CHAPTER 38

Don took Leanne's hands and placed them close to his heart. Filled with emotion, he could barely whisper, "Please, Leanne, will you marry me . . . be my wife again? I love you and need you. I love you, want you back. Please say yes."

"Yes, Don," she said, her voice soft and intimate. "I will always be your wife. I've *never* stopped loving you."

He put his arms around her, and she clasped his head with both her hands, bringing his face close to hers. When their lips met, it was with the same sweetness and tenderness that was so familiar to them. They clung together, as if fearing separation. Don was like a drowning man, gasping for air as he rained kisses all over Leanne's face. She moaned in his arms, her whole body shaking with deep emotion.

"Leanne, I'm, I'm so sor—"

"Shh, shh," she said, placing her forefinger against his lips to stop his apology. "It's all right."

Don hoped that the craziness he had gone through was over. He was where he belonged, in the arms of the woman he truly loved.

"Forgive me, Leanne, please."

Again she silenced his plea, placing her whole hand over his mouth.

Still clinging to one another, they rose from the sofa and wordlessly walked upstairs to Leanne's room.

Fully clothed, they collapsed on the bed. Not a word passed between them, as each knew what the other wanted.

Don began to undress Leanne as she tugged at his clothing, each afraid to stop until their bodies were free.

Like tentative newlyweds, they touched, explored, frantically nuzzled each other as if they had never been apart. The loving gestures, touching sensations were as before. Their bodies reacted as the sweet memories of the past returned.

Several months later.

The wedding took place in the family court judge's chambers.

The bride was radiant in a white silk Chanel suit, and the groom, his dark hair showing twin patches of silver at the temples, was handsome in a gray suit with satin lapels.

Their son was the best man and their daughter the maid of honor.

With Don formally agreeing to Jay's adoption, Bob had been allowed to adopt his son, renamed John Matthews Sato. "Just my son," he declared to anyone who asked.

At the ceremony were Bob's brothers, Caleb and Morris, and his parents, whom Don and Leanne had yet to meet.

Jane's fiancé, Sam Adams, was present as well.

The elder Satos were the first to congratulate the couple after the simple ceremony.

Herman Sato bowed low in front of Don before extending his hand.

"My sincere good wishes, sir," he said.

"Thank you, Mr. Sato. I am so happy to meet you and your wife," Don said. Then he said to the pair, "May I present my wife, Leanne Matthews?"

"It's a pleasure to meet you, Mrs. Matthews. And I want to thank you for helping my son, Bob." Belinda smiled.

"I was very happy to help him. He is a wonderful young man, and I know you are happy and very proud of him, as you should be.

"The whole family is," Belinda Sato said. "To us, always it's the family that matters."

"You are so right, Mrs. Sato. I'm very happy, feel blessed to have *my* family."

Then she turned to Herman Sato. "You are coming to our house for a small reception, aren't you? We'd love to have you meet some of our friends, since you are new to the area."

Mr. Sato bowed deeply once again. "Yes, we are most pleased to come, Mrs. Matthews."

Linking her arm with her husband's arm, Leanne replied, "We are delighted to share this day with you."

Don, nodding in agreement, offering his hand to Mr. Sato, said, "My wife couldn't have said it better. I agree with her wholeheartedly."

EPILOGUE

By July Cornwallis Farley was glad to be on vacation. She had finished a very busy year teaching the graduate nursing students and was thrilled to have this week at her time-share condo in Aruba.

As soon as she unpacked her clothes, she made a pitcher of iced tea. She poured a glass for herself, placed the pitcher back in the refrigerator, picked up her sunglasses and her newest book, and headed out to the deck.

She placed her drink on a small table, sat down in her chaise lounge, sighed deeply and closed her eyes for a moment. She felt the almost unbearable tension begin to leave her body. She relaxed in the warm sun. The ocean's waves thundered on the shoreline and the repetitive sounds made her relax.

"Hello, there! It's nice to see you. When did you get in?"

Wally looked over the railing and saw Becky Long smiling at her from the adjoining deck.

"Oh, hi. I'm glad to see you, Becky . . . Becky Long, is it?"

"Right. How *are* you?"

"Good. Real good. Just got in today and I'm so glad to be here."

"Know what you mean. John and I have been here for a few days, and we're having a great time."

"I'm looking forward to some relaxation myself. I really need it."

"Don't we all?" Becky said.

"Becky, didn't you tell me that you worked for a Dr. Matthews?"

"I still do. Why do you ask?"

"When we first met, I was sharing a condo with a girl named Alisha Morton."

Becky plopped down in a chair and rested her arms on the railing to stare at her neighbor.

"You lie!"

"No, I'm not lying . . ."

"That girl! I tried to warn her, but she had set her mind on Dr. Matthews. Poor man, he had no chance!"

"So she married him?"

"Told him she was carrying his child! He divorced his wife of twenty-five years and married her."

"Well, when I found out what she was up to, I just couldn't live with her anymore, so we sold the condo and parted ways. Is she still with him?"

"Wallis, girl," Becky's voice was pitched low and she gave her answer in a deliberately paced fashion for maximum effect.

"*Wally, that bitch tricked him. She had used a sperm donor. Told him it was his!*"

"Oh, my God! She is crazy!"

"Tell me about it."

"What happened?"

"I guess being a physician, he suspected something after the child was born. Had a DNA test done that proved the child was not his."

"Then what?"

"Oh, he divorced her. The child was adopted and he and his ex-wife remarried."

"Why on earth would his wife take him back after all that?"

"She loved him."

THE END

2010 Mass Market Titles

January

Show Me The Sun
Miriam Shumba
ISBN: 978-158571-405-6
$6.99

Promises of Forever
Celya Bowers
ISBN: 978-1-58571-380-6
$6.99

February

Love Out Of Order
Nicole Green
ISBN: 978-1-58571-381-3
$6.99

Unclear and Present Danger
Michele Cameron
ISBN: 978-158571-408-7
$6.99

March

Stolen Jewels
Michele Sudler
ISBN: 978-158571-409-4
$6.99

Not Quite Right
Tammy Williams
ISBN: 978-158571-410-0
$6.99

April

Oak Bluffs
Joan Early
ISBN: 978-1-58571-379-0
$6.99

Crossing The Line
Bernice Layton
ISBN: 978-158571-412-4
$6.99

How To Kill Your Husband
Keith Walker
ISBN: 978-158571-421-6
$6.99

May

The Business of Love
Cheris F. Hodges
ISBN: 978-158571-373-8
$6.99

Wayward Dreams
Gail McFarland
ISBN: 978-158571-422-3
$6.99

June

The Doctor's Wife
Mildred Riley
ISBN: 978-158571-424-7
$6.99

Mixed Reality
Chamein Canton
ISBN: 978-158571-423-0
$6.99

2010 Mass Market Titles (continued)
July

Blue Interlude
Keisha Mennefee
ISBN: 978-158571-378-3
$6.99

Always You
Crystal Hubbard
ISBN: 978-158571-371-4
$6.99

Unbeweavable
Katrina Spencer
ISBN: 978-158571-426-1
$6.99

August

Small Sensations
Crystal V. Rhodes
ISBN: 978-158571-376-9
$6.99

Let's Get It On
Dyanne Davis
ISBN: 978-158571-416-2
$6.99

September

Unconditional
A.C. Arthur
ISBN: 978-158571-413-1
$6.99

Swan
Africa Fine
ISBN: 978-158571-377-6
$6.99$6.99

October

Friends in Need
Joan Early
ISBN:978-1-58571-428-5
$6.99

Against the Wind
Gwynne Forster
ISBN:978-158571-429-2
$6.99

That Which Has Horns
Miriam Shumba
ISBN:978-1-58571-430-8
$6.99

November

A Good Dude
Keith Walker
ISBN:978-1-58571-431-5
$6.99

Reye's Gold
Ruthie Robinson
ISBN:978-1-58571-432-2
$6.99

December

Still Waters...
Crystal V. Rhodes
ISBN:978-1-58571-433-9
$6.99

Burn
Crystal Hubbard
ISBN: 978-1-58571-406-3
$6.99

Other Genesis Press, Inc. Titles

Other Genesis Press, Inc. Titles (continued)

Other Genesis Press, Inc. Titles (continued)

Eve's Prescription	Edwina Martin Arnold	$8.95
Everlastin' Love	Gay G. Gunn	$8.95
Everlasting Moments	Dorothy Elizabeth Love	$8.95
Everything and More	Sinclair Lebeau	$8.95
Everything But Love	Natalie Dunbar	$8.95
Falling	Natalie Dunbar	$9.95
Fate	Pamela Leigh Starr	$8.95
Finding Isabella	A.J. Garrotto	$8.95
Fireflies	Joan Early	$6.99
Fixin' Tyrone	Keith Walker	$6.99
Forbidden Quest	Dar Tomlinson	$10.95
Forever Love	Wanda Y. Thomas	$8.95
From the Ashes	Kathleen Suzanne	$8.95
	Jeanne Sumerix	
Frost On My Window	Angela Weaver	$6.99
Gentle Yearning	Rochelle Alers	$10.95
Glory of Love	Sinclair LeBeau	$10.95
Go Gentle Into That	Malcom Boyd	$12.95
Good Night		
Goldengroove	Mary Beth Craft	$16.95
Groove, Bang, and Jive	Steve Cannon	$8.99
Hand In Glove	Andrea Jackson	$9.95
Hard to Love	Kimberley White	$9.95
Hart & Soul	Angie Daniels	$8.95
Heart of the Phoenix	A.C. Arthur	$9.95
Heartbeat	Stephanie Bedwell-Grime	$8.95
Hearts Remember	M. Loui Quezada	$8.95
Hidden Memories	Robin Allen	$10.95
Higher Ground	Leah Latimer	$19.95
Hitler, the War, and the Pope	Ronald Rychiak	$26.95
How to Write a Romance	Kathryn Falk	$18.95
I Married a Reclining Chair	Lisa M. Fuhs	$8.95
I'll Be Your Shelter	Giselle Carmichael	$8.95
I'll Paint a Sun	A.J. Garrotto	$9.95
Icie	Pamela Leigh Starr	$8.95
If I Were Your Woman	LaConnie Taylor-Jones	$6.99
Illusions	Pamela Leigh Starr	$8.95
Indigo After Dark Vol. I	Nia Dixon/Angelique	$10.95
Indigo After Dark Vol. II	Dolores Bundy/	$10.95
	Cole Riley	
Indigo After Dark Vol. III	Montana Blue/	$10.95
	Coco Morena	

Other Genesis Press, Inc. Titles (continued)

Other Genesis Press, Inc. Titles (continued)

Other Genesis Press, Inc. Titles (continued)

Other Genesis Press, Inc. Titles (continued)

The Missing Link	Charlyne Dickerson	$8.95
The Mission	Pamela Leigh Starr	$6.99
The More Things Change	Chamein Canton	$6.99
The Perfect Frame	Beverly Clark	$9.95
The Price of Love	Sinclair LeBeau	$8.95
The Smoking Life	Ilene Barth	$29.95
The Words of the Pitcher	Kei Swanson	$8.95
Things Forbidden	Maryam Diaab	$6.99
This Life Isn't Perfect Holla	Sandra Foy	$6.99
Three Doors Down	Michele Sudler	$6.99
Three Wishes	Seressia Glass	$8.95
Ties That Bind	Kathleen Suzanne	$8.95
Tiger Woods	Libby Hughes	$5.95
Time Is of the Essence	Angie Daniels	$9.95
Timeless Devotion	Bella McFarland	$9.95
Tomorrow's Promise	Leslie Esdaile	$8.95
Truly Inseparable	Wanda Y. Thomas	$8.95
Two Sides to Every Story	Dyanne Davis	$9.95
Unbreak My Heart	Dar Tomlinson	$8.95
Uncommon Prayer	Kenneth Swanson	$9.95
Unconditional Love	Alicia Wiggins	$8.95
Unconditional	A.C. Arthur	$9.95
Undying Love	Renee Alexis	$6.99
Until Death Do Us Part	Susan Paul	$8.95
Vows of Passion	Bella McFarland	$9.95
Waiting for Mr. Darcy	Chamein Canton	$6.99
Waiting in the Shadows	Michele Sudler	$6.99
Wedding Gown	Dyanne Davis	$8.95
What's Under Benjamin's Bed	Sandra Schaffer	$8.95
When a Man Loves a Woman	LaConnie Taylor-Jones	$6.99
When Dreams Float	Dorothy Elizabeth Love	$8.95
When I'm With You	LaConnie Taylor-Jones	$6.99
When Lightning Strikes	Michele Cameron	$6.99
Where I Want To Be	Maryam Diaab	$6.99
Whispers In the Night	Dorothy Elizabeth Love	$8.95
Whispers in the Sand	LaFlorya Gauthier	$10.95
Who's That Lady?	Andrea Jackson	$9.95
Wild Ravens	AlTonya Washington	$9.95
Yesterday Is Gone	Beverly Clark	$10.95
Yesterday's Dreams, Tomorrow's Promises	Reon Laudat	$8.95
Your Precious Love	Sinclair LeBeau	$8.95

Order Form

Mail to: Genesis Press, Inc.
P.O. Box 101
Columbus, MS 39703

Name _____
Address _____
City/State _____ Zip _____
Telephone _____

Ship to (if different from above)
Name _____
Address _____
City/State _____ Zip _____
Telephone _____

Credit Card Information
Credit Card # _____ ☐ Visa   ☐ Mastercard
Expiration Date (mm/yy) _____ ☐ AmEx   ☐ Discover

Qty.	Author	Title	Price	Total

Use this order form, or call 1-888-INDIGO-1	Total for books _____
	Shipping and handling:
	$5 first two books,
	$1 each additional book _____
	Total S & H _____
	Total amount enclosed _____
	Mississippi residents add 7% sales tax